CW00517946

THE SPARE ROOM

M. I. HATTERSLEY

DARK CORRIDOR BOOKS

GET YOUR FREE THRILLER

To show my appreciation to you for buying this book I'd like to invite you to join my exclusive Readers Club and receive a free copy of my novel, *The Ex*.

What if your ex's former lovers were all dying in mysterious circumstances and you were next on the list?

To get your free novel click here:

https://www.mihattersley.com/freebook

ONE

I can't hear. I can't see.

I clamber to my feet and stumble forward as an intense wave of adrenaline surges through my system. My hands are shaking. My legs don't work properly. I have an overriding impulse to run as fast as I can in any direction but I'm certain if I try I'll fall over.

Where is Graham?

I just want Graham.

I need someone here who loves me and cares for me.

I need someone to wrap their arms around me and tell me everything is going to be all right.

What the hell is going on?

My mind feels like a jigsaw puzzle that has been smashed into its component parts. I have snippets of ideas and images in my head but none of them fit together, and some are upside down so I can only see their shape and not how they fit into the overall picture. The rest is just fog. I need to think straight. I need to work out what's going on. But my head is full of noise.

As I stumble towards the light I can see movement, people. Most of them are shouting and waving their arms. They look angry. Some of them are wearing uniforms.

Of course. The police. That's why I'm here.

The realisation sends a nausea response rushing to my guts. I heave but manage to hold it in and raise my hands in the air. That seems to be what they're asking me to do. I open my mouth to speak. So I can tell them who I am. But my throat is so dry I can't form words.

Why are they still shouting at me? Their words are muffled and disjointed and I can't make out what they're saying.

"Get her away…"

"Someone grab her…"

I move closer to the lights and it's as if I'm floating. I feel detached from my own body as if I'm watching a news report of what's going on rather than being here. This has happened to me before. It's a shock response to trauma, a way of disconnecting from events so you can survive.

And that's me. A survivor.

It's all I've ever been.

But all I can think right now is, this is bad. This is very bad. This shouldn't be happening. I screw my eyes up to try to recall what happened and what I should do now. I'm shaking and shivering and all I want is to be far, far away from here. Somewhere safe. But the police are here.

That's a good thing.

Isn't it?

As my jittery awareness begins to stabilise, I open my eyes wide and glance around. I'm in the forecourt of a large warehouse which is surrounded by a tall metal fence. Over to my right are more large buildings and beyond these an urban landscape of high-rise office blocks. To my left, the scene opens out to the inky night sky and what looks like water. I was here. I am here. I feel the concrete ground under my feet as I stumble forward. Through the lights I see someone step towards me. They're waving at me, beckoning me forth.

I stumble as the world rushes into focus at my feet. That's when I see them. Two of them. A man and a woman. They're both lying on the ground. Him on his front. Her on her back. Neither of them is moving and, as I watch, people wearing dark clothes rush over to them.

But I can tell they're dead. They're both dead.

As if from nowhere, an intense swell of rage overcomes me. I try to scream, to release the pressure in my head. I'm not sure if I manage it.

There is more shouting and waving of arms. I wipe at my eyes to try and disperse the fog clouding my vision. My face is wet with sweat. I hold my fingers up in front of my face, widening my eyes to better focus. But it's not sweat on my face. It's blood.

My blood? Their blood?

I tense and pull my arms into my chest as a figure rushes towards me holding their arms out. I think they're speaking to me, but I still can't make out what they're saying.

How did it get to this?

I was only supposed to be here doing my damn course. This isn't me. This isn't who I am. Not anymore. Maybe not ever. I know I've done bad things in my life. Awful things. But you can't blame someone for reacting to the circumstances in which they find themselves.

This was a mistake. I shouldn't be here. I want to be back home. I want to be in Oxford with Graham. I was safe there. Why did it have to end?

Why does everything always have to end?

TWO

FOUR DAYS EARLIER

Something feels wrong. Normally, I'm good at reading situations. I've had to be. When you have the sort of past I have, you need all your wits about you. Now, though, my gut is telling me to turn around.

I take a step backwards so I can get a better view of the Victorian terraced house in front of me. It doesn't look like it did on the email I was sent and to say it looks run down would be an understatement. Moss has grown over the tops of bricks and whole sections are missing on some of them, exposing crumbling mortar underneath. One of the wooden windows is rotten at the corner, paint flaking away from its frame. The front door is worse; it's covered in a layer of grime and parts of the plastic number forty-seven that adorns the top right-hand corner have chipped away.

I grip the handle of my suitcase as I glance up and down the street. I'm aware the small town of Market Allerton, isn't the most affluent of locations but the place gives me the creeps. Down at the end of the street, a dark figure with a dog appears under a lamp post and stops to let him do his business. He must see me too because he turns his head towards me for a moment before moving on up ahead. I can't make out his face or even if he's looking at me, but I feel a shiver run down my spine all the same. It might be the fact that winter is around the corner and it's a cold night. It also got very dark on the bus ride over here.

I roll my shoulders back and turn my attention back to the house. Gut feelings aside, it could just be the cold and the dark getting to me. It wouldn't be the first time my overactive imagination has been my undoing. In the day, in the sunshine, this street and this house probably seem fine. Plus, there's nothing specific I can put my finger on as to why I'm feeling anxious. It's more than likely just stress and fatigue making me jumpy.

I pull out my phone to check the time, dismayed to see it is past seven-thirty. The email that Rochelle forwarded to me said I had to be here by seven. I swipe open my phone display and go into my emails. The confirmation from the *VayCay Rooms* website that Rochelle sent over is near the top of the list. I click on it, despite having checked it three times on the journey over here. But the address is correct. This is the right house. So why doesn't it look right? I consider going on the site to double-check, but the signal has dropped. I'm only getting that weird 'E' in place of where the phone usually tells me it's connected to '4G'. Does anyone know even what that E stands for?

Empty?

Exasperating?

Extremely annoying?

Regardless, it is the right address – 47 Cranbourne Street - and I could catch a cold if I stand outside any longer. I wish work had booked me in somewhere a little nicer, but I'm aware it was last minute and was probably cheap. Besides, it's only for five nights and I'll hardly be here for most of the time. It'll serve its purpose. Even if it's not anywhere near as luxurious or pretty as the palatial surroundings of Samstone Manor.

An uncomfortable feeling of resentment and remorse tightens the muscles in my face. Samstone Manor is the venue for the five-day course in Human Resources Management, that I'm here in town to attend. The large stately home is a twenty-five-minute drive from Market Allerton and course attendees are usually put up in one of the manor's many bedrooms, but as I was enrolled on the course late it was booked up. Just my luck. Rochelle in HR booked this place for me yesterday morning. She said it looked decent and I did see some photos, but they must have been taken a long time ago.

But at least I'm here. And at least I will have a job at the end of this. Once I qualify, I'll have the opportunity for growth and be able to move up the corporate ladder at GP Telecom. That's what Rochelle has told me, anyway. I'm still undecided whether that's what I actually want. But right now I'm not sure about so many aspects of my life. A lot has happened to me recently.

Sucking in a deep breath I open the gate and walk up to the front door. The house is set back from the pavement, but I wouldn't call the metre-wide strip of concrete in front of the window a garden. You see this a lot in old terraces, especially in the Midlands and up north. It gives the impression there's a front garden – and this area is probably described as such by estate agents – but it's far too narrow to fit even the daintiest of patio furniture. You might get a few pots in here in which to plant flowers. But, looking around, none of the houses on this street have gone for this option. In fact, I can't see any flowers anywhere. There is no colour on the street at all. Not even a brightly painted front door. In the low moonlight, all I can see are shades of beige and terracotta, all filtered through the blue-black hue of night. I suppose it's similar to the street I grew up on. Although I don't remember much about that time.

The curtains are drawn across the front window, allowing only a dull glow from inside to escape. It looks cosy enough. According to Rochelle, I've got a self-contained room on the first floor but will have to share a bathroom. It's not ideal but Market Allerton is hardly a tourist spot so it's not in anyone's interest to spend lots of money presenting somewhere like the Ritz. The people who stay here are most likely people like me-here on business and needing somewhere cheap and cheerful for a few nights. It'll be fine, I tell myself.

I reach up and knock on the door before shuffling back a little way. While I wait, I open up my emails once more, so I have the confirmation ready to show whoever is here to let me in. Straightening my back as I hear movement on the other side of the door, I force a smile onto my face. A moment later I hear a bolt lock being slid open followed by a key turning in a lock.

"Oh? Hello there."

I'm expecting someone younger and more professional-looking, so when an old man wearing an out-of-shape burgundy cardigan and a confused expression opens the door I'm rather taken aback. The sleeves of the cardigan are frayed, and there is a hole in one elbow that reveals a circle of pale skin. His sparse white hair sticks up at random angles from his head like it hasn't seen a comb in weeks. He eyes me, suspiciously.

"Hello there," he says. "What do you want?"

I tense. Have I got the wrong house? I want to check again, but that's ridiculous. I know this is the right house. Still, it doesn't stop me from rereading the confirmation email for the tenth time.

But yes. I'm right.

Come on, girl.

Trust yourself a bit more.

"My name's Lauren Williams," I say. "I've got a room booked here for the next five nights."

I phrase my last words with a questioning intonation, hoping to get an affirmative response. To further push him towards a positive reaction, I nod eagerly and give him an encouraging smile. Unfortunately, he just stands still in the doorway with a puzzled look on his face.

What the hell is going on?

I sense my benign smile morphing into one more desperate and rictus-like with every second.

"I'm sorry that I'm late," I continue. "It's my fault. I should have messaged you to let you know I wouldn't be here for seven. It's been a bit of a whirlwind for me the last couple of days, truth be told. I do apologise for the oversight. But I'm here now. This is 47 Cranbourne Street, isn't it?" I hold up my phone to show him the email.

"That's right." He narrows his eyes at the screen and the sagging skin around his jowls shudders as he mouths the words to himself. "You're staying here, are you?"

"Yes. My colleague has booked the room for me, via the VayCay Rooms website." I feel my chest tightening. "You do have a room available?"

"We've got a few," he says, with a slight chuckle. "What did you say your name was again, love?"

"Lauren," I tell him.

Is he going to let me in?

He still doesn't move. He appears friendly, though. I

always take a good look into people's eyes when I first meet them. It's something I've done since I was little. You can usually tell what someone is like just by looking at their eyes; I can, anyway. This man's eyes are the lightest shade of blue and have a watery look, but there's kindness in them. And it hits me that I haven't even asked him his name. "Sorry. And you are?"

He smiles and his face lights up. "They call me—"

"Ron!? Who is it?"

The old man startles at the sound of a woman's voice coming from the hallway behind him. A second later the owner of the voice appears and shoves past him.

"Hello, dear," she says, on seeing me. "I'm Peggy. How are you?"

Peggy is at least a foot shorter than Ron, who I assume is her husband. She's slim and small-framed, but very sturdy-looking the way some old women are. Her wavy hair is dyed a light auburn colour and the way it's combed back, it resembles an orange halo surrounding her lined face. She, too, has kind eyes and a pleasant smile, but I can't help feeling weirded out by the old couple.

It's only because I was expecting someone younger, I tell myself.

It's not a big deal.

Peggy raises her eyebrows at me as if waiting for my response and I splutter out the same introduction I gave Ron, telling her my name and that I'm booked into one of their rooms for five nights.

"You do have a room?" I ask, once again holding up my phone like it's the oracle of all truth.

Peggy doesn't look at the screen but nods. "Of course we do."

"Thank God." I sense the muscles of my neck and shoulders relax. "I was beginning to think something had gone wrong."

"Pay no attention to Ron," Peggy says, ushering the old man back into the gloom of the house. When he wanders off down the hallway, she rolls her eyes at me and smiles as if to say '*Men!*' "Look at you, aren't you pretty."

I laugh and look away. "Oh, I don't know about that. I'm tired and weary from the bus."

"Gosh, yes. What am I thinking," Peggy says, stepping back and beckoning me inside. "Come in. We've got everything set out for you."

"Excellent. Thank you," I say and, despite the apprehensive feeling in the pit of my stomach, I pick up my suitcase and step inside.

THREE

I used to trust my instincts more than anything else in the world. They were all I had to go on. Listening to them, and heeding them, has got me out of a lot of scrapes over the years. But over the last eighteen months, I've realised I can't even trust my gut any longer. What is it they say about pride coming before a fall? I was such a fool to believe everything was going well for me. But it looked that way. My life was on the up. After years of living life on a knife edge, not knowing where I would be from one month to the next, I felt as if I was finally on firm ground. I no longer had to exist in flight mode, unable to settle in any one place in case something awful happened and I had to leave. After meeting Graham, I actually allowed myself to relax. For the first time ever. I was content. Happy, even. It was a strange and slightly unsettling feeling, but I loved it all the same. I had everything I'd ever wanted. A nice house. Someone who loved me and cared for me.

Or so I thought.

Which is why I don't trust my instincts any longer. The

sense of unease, as I step into the house and Peggy locks the front door behind me feels real enough, but I've been so wrong in the past.

But why should I be worried? I'm only going to be here for a few nights. Even though the house and situation are not exactly what I had hoped, Peggy and Ron seem nice enough. Furthermore, they're both elderly and slightly hunched over. Peggy's fingers are crooked and arthritic. Surely neither of them poses much of a threat.

"Do you both live here?" I ask as Peggy wanders down the gloomy hallway in front of me.

She smiles and nods at me. "That's right, dear."

The house smells…old and I can't help but think that a bit of light would do wonders for the place. Perhaps they're trying to save money on their electricity bill. Although, from how hot and stuffy the house is I'd say turning their radiators down would be more beneficial. To my right is a staircase leading upwards while two doors on my left presumably lead to the front room and dining room. At the end of the corridor, directly in front of me, is a kitchen - likely an extension. I lived somewhere like this for a while when I was fourteen: same floorplan, same kitchen extension. It's a classic Victorian terrace layout.

Peggy stops at the first door and frowns. "We've been here almost sixty years. It was me and Ron for a long time. Then our little Charlotte came along. Come and have a sit-down."

"Oh, I see. No," I glance down at my suitcase propped on its wheels beside me. "I won't if that's okay. It's been a long day. I think I need to have a wash and get ready for bed. If you wouldn't mind showing me to my room, I'll…"

I trail off as Peggy disappears into the room beyond. Despite my fatigue and desire to get unpacked and prepare for tomorrow I leave my case in the hallway and follow her through.

"Sit down," she says. "You must be tired out, you poor duck."

I cast my attention around the room. Ron is sitting in a dark green armchair in the corner facing a television that isn't switched on. He doesn't look up as I enter and side-step over to the matching dark green sofa which is against the wall next to the door. Peggy nods at me as if offering encouragement and I sit. Opposite the sofa is an ornately tiled fireplace with an electric three-bar fire sitting on the hearth. The mantelpiece above displays a selection of photographs in silver frames. My eyes land on an old black and white shot of two people getting married which I assume to be Peggy and Ron. Next to this is a colour photograph of a young girl of about nine or ten with blonde wavy hair and freckles. Despite the ageing décor, it's a nice enough front room but something about it bothers me and I can't quite work out what it is.

"Now then, a cup of tea?" Peggy asks.

"No. Thank you. I'm fine."

"Ah. That's a shame." She smiles and nods some more. I smile back. "Isn't she pretty, Ron? What did you say your name was again?"

"Lauren," I tell her. "Lauren Williams. You were expecting me, weren't you? The website should have sent confirmation through - and I believe my employers have already settled the bill."

Mentioning money feels awkward, but I want to get it out there early and confirm I don't owe anything for my stay. Moving into my new flat in Manchester has drained almost all of my savings. Once I gain this certification my new salary will leave me comfortable, but I won't receive my first pay check until the end of next month. That's the downside of beginning a job in the middle of a pay period.

"Lauren. That's right." Peggy chuckles to herself. "And you're staying for a week?"

"Five nights."

Bloody hell.

This doesn't bode well. I'm hoping there's someone else around here who knows what's going on more than these old dears. Charlotte, perhaps. The daughter.

Peggy raises a finger in the air. "I remember. Five nights. Sorry, ducky. I do get a bit hazy the later it gets in the day. But don't you worry about a thing. Everything you need is taken care of. There's a nice room upstairs waiting for you and we'll look after you while you're staying here. Won't we, Ron?"

I smile. "Thank you."

"Have you come far?" she asks, loitering in the middle of the room and wringing her bony hands together.

"From Manchester," I say. "But I had to catch two buses to get here because of the train strikes. That's why I'm a bit late."

That shows how well I'm handling life right now. My head is still in bits after the breakup, so I didn't even realise there was industrial action taking place until I got to the train station. Apparently, the strikes have been all over the news for weeks. I never even noticed.

"You poor thing," Peggy says, tilting her head to one side with a smile. I wish she'd stop looking at me the way she is doing. She's making me uncomfortable. "Let me make you a sandwich?"

"No. I'm fine."

"Some toast?"

I hold my hand up. "Really. I'm good." I didn't expect a welcome party. I certainly didn't expect anyone to provide food. This trend of letting out of your spare rooms to guests is new to me but I don't think meal provision is a usual occurrence. I know Peggy is just being friendly, but wish it was just Charlotte or whoever meeting me to hand over the keys. I could do without the third degree. She's still looking at me with a concerned expression. Is this what she does with all her guests? Do people appreciate her being this way? "I've already eaten," I add. "But thank you."

"A cup of tea then? I was boiling the kettle anyway when you arrived."

"No. I already said—" I stop myself and take a deep breath.

She's from a different generation, Lauren.

She only wants to be a good host.

"A cup of tea will be lovely," I say.

Peggy brightens at this and as she smiles, she reminds me of Nana Mary. It's the way her eyes crinkle up at the corners and the way she bunches her shoulders. I haven't thought about Nana Mary in years and the similarity to her warms me to Peggy even more. I'm still thinking about the old days when she scuttles out of the room, leaving me alone with Ron.

I sigh and clear my throat, expecting him to look over, but he remains staring at the blank tv screen. I wonder what he's thinking about as I, too, stare into the black rectangle. Is he thinking about anything? Should I make conversation? It's the last thing I feel like doing but I am a guest here and it's important to be polite. I've had that drummed into me so many times over the years I can't bring myself to not be.

"Do you want me to switch it on for you?" I ask him.

He doesn't respond. I sit back and glance around the room, nodding and smiling, smiling and nodding. What do I do now? I'm assuming my room is on the first floor. As soon as Peggy gets back with the tea, I'll ask if I can take it up with me.

I'm also assuming that after this introductory meeting, I'll be left to my own devices by and large. That better be the case. I might value politeness but there is a limit.

"How old are you?"

The question catches me off guard, as does the way Ron barks it at me across the room. I'm a little embarrassed at the fact I visibly jump but laugh to cover it.

"Me? Oh, I'm twenty-eight," I reply.

"You look younger."

"Thank you. I think."

"Our Charlotte is twenty-eight," he says and looks proud at himself for remembering. Maybe if you get to Ron's age you take what you can. I've not been around old people for several years so I can't remember what's normal. But he seems incredibly forgetful and distant. None of this helps the weird, unsettling feeling that's still lying heavy on my stomach. Nor does the fact the house is so still and silent.

"Does she live here, too?" I ask.

He scowls as if thinking about it. "She used to. But she moved away. She went to university."

"Ah I see."

"Liverpool. That's where she is."

"Ah, lovely. I've never been. I should visit though, now I'm living up here. I hear it's a lovely city."

I only moved to Manchester from Oxford five weeks ago, so my feet have yet to properly hit the ground, but once they do I intend to explore the area. Having lived in the south of England my whole life, my hope is this new environment will be good for me. I don't know anyone up here but, likewise, no one knows me. That's a good thing.

The rattle of crockery coming from the hallway has me sitting up straight and I twist around in my seat to see Peggy enter carrying a tray containing a teapot and three mugs. None of the crockery matches and for some reason, I find comfort in that. These are real people. Nice people. It's a strange place I've found myself in, but what if this is exactly what I need right now?

And yes, the accommodation is far from the luxury I was hoping for when Rochelle told me I'd be staying over for the five nights of the course - but it's important not to hold onto your expectations too tightly. The minute you set your desires in stone, you're really only setting yourself up to get hurt. The thing you wanted the most doesn't happen, or it happens and isn't what you thought it was going to be, or it happens but is somehow off-kilter anyway and makes you wish even more fervently that it would never have happened so that you wouldn't have lost the lovely illusion of perfect bliss in your mind's eye.

So, screw it. The area is a little creepy and Peggy and Ron are rather old and odd, but I'll hardly see much of them after tonight. And it's only five days.

"What have you two been gabbing about?" Peggy asks, placing the tray down on a small coffee table near the sofa and passing me a mug of tea.

"Ron was just telling me about your daughter, Charlotte."

Peggy beams at this. "She's a nurse. She lives in Liverpool."

"So I hear."

Peggy glances over at Ron but he's back staring at the TV. I wonder if he's got some sort of degenerative disease like Alzheimer's or similar. It would make a lot of sense. But why advertise your spare room on VayCay Rooms if you aren't well? Surely it creates a lot of undue stress and upheaval having new guests come through here on a weekly basis.

"Do you have a lot of people staying here?" I ask.

"Oh, yes," Peggy says. "It's nice to have people in the house again. And the money helps."

Her smile drops suddenly and I sense a deep sadness coming from her. It must be awful to reach her age and still have money troubles, to the point you have to open part of your home to strangers. I never want to get into that position. But that's why I'm here, staying in a strange house in a strange town so I can get my HR qualification and start climbing the corporate ladder to the stars. Or to utter boredom and the death of my soul. Whichever comes first.

I sip at my tea. It's far too weak for my taste and the water doesn't feel as if it's reached boiling point. I rest the mug on my knee.

"Anyway, I am rather tired," I say, grimacing. "Would it be okay if you showed me to my room? I'd like to get settled and prepare for tomorrow. I've got a rather early start."

Peggy's eyes widen but she shrugs in a friendly enough way. "Yes, you must be shattered, you poor love. I'll show you up there now."

The tension I've been holding in my chest drops away. "Awesome. Thank you." Peggy gets to her feet and so do I, handing her the mug which she places back on the tray.

"If you want to follow me, I'll give you a quick tour and show you where everything is," she says.

I step back to let her leave the room first and give Ron a wave as I follow her out. At the door, it hits me what's been troubling me about the room. On the website, there were photos of the room I'd be renting, but there were also a few of the main house. I remember now there was a shot of the front room. It was laid out pretty much the same as this one, but I remember the room in the photo was painted white and this one has pale pink wallpaper on the walls.

I stop and spin around, ready to ask Peggy about the discrepancy, but she's already on her way upstairs. I shake the thought away. It's probably nothing. The wallpaper does look rather new. More than likely, they had it put up since the photo was taken.

But I can't shake this uneasy feeling that I should leave this house right now. No matter how late it is or how cold outside I should grab my suitcase and get out of here. But I know I can't. Work has booked this accommodation for me and the last thing I want to do is be labelled a trouble causer before I even properly start at the company. I have to make a good impression. Show them I'm as resilient and open-minded as I made out in my interview. So, I push these thoughts to one side and tell myself I'm being silly. Besides, instincts can be deceiving and I can't trust my gut.

I've been so wrong in the past.

FOUR

As I grab my case and follow Peggy upstairs one thought keeps going over and over in my head.

This is not what I signed up for.

The stairs creak and groan beneath my feet as we climb. There are more photographs hanging from the wall, in the same silver frames as downstairs. Memories of Peggy and Ron's life. The two of them by a lake, Peggy holding a newborn baby in her arms, Ron in a restaurant with a young girl - presumably Charlotte - sitting on his lap and making a stupid face. I take in the pictures but don't really process them. I'm too busy wondering if I should say something to Peggy and try to rectify a few of my concerns.

But what do I say?

That the accommodation isn't up to my expectations.

That I was hoping I'd get the keys to my room stuffed in my hand and left to my own devices.

I've no idea how to broach either of these subjects without it sounding incredibly rude and insulting to the meek old woman with the kind smile who is waiting for me as I reach the landing. It smells funny up here, sort of musty and old. I inhale a deep breath to try and work out what it is but can't pinpoint any one particular smell. It reminds me of charity shops and libraries but I'm not sure either of those things is recognised as scent notes.

"You are such a pretty young thing," Peggy says as I step up to join her.

That's another thing that's creeping me out a little about being here. I wish she'd stop saying things like that to me. I am pretty, I know that. Men have told me it all my life. But you get to a point when you want to be recognised for more than what you look like. Especially as most people who've ever said that to me wanted something in return. But I know Peggy's not like that. And she does seem genuine.

"Thank you," I say. "Charlotte is very pretty too, I notice. From the photos. She looks a lot like you when you were young."

Despite my reservations, I do know how to talk to people when I want them to like me. Kids who are from a similar background to mine seem to go one of two ways. They either draw into themselves and become anti-social and reclusive, or they learn how to charm people in the hope those people will care for them. It was an instinctive choice back when I was too young to make it of course, but I'm glad I took the latter path. It's been a lot easier this way. It got me a good job, friends, a nice fiancé. For a while at least.

And Peggy seems to enjoy the compliment if her girlish giggle is anything to go by. She steps towards me and lowers her voice. "I am sorry about Ron," she says. "He's a good man and wouldn't harm a fly, but he can get a bit forgetful these days."

I step back. "Oh? I see."

I'd also wager that '*a bit forgetful*' is a contender for under-statement of the year, but I don't say anything. She's playing his condition down, maybe for my benefit, maybe for hers. It can't be easy caring for your husband while his mind wastes away. But that's love, I suppose. Forget flowers and romantic gestures. Find yourself someone ready to wipe your arse and spoon-feed you soup in your old age. But then, Peggy strikes me as being rather vague and forgetful also. What was it she said about the night-time making her hazy? Maybe she's taken primary care of Ron because she's scared of being on her own. Or she doesn't remember how to be.

I feel rotten for thinking all this. She's old and lovely and clearly wants to make me feel welcome. I'm being a bitch. I need to stop.

I focus on Peggy's face in an attempt to stay present. She has green-brown eyes which, even though magnified by her thick spectacles, are almost lost under the folds of skin over her eyelids. Her cheeks and jawline are a map of tiny lines and crevasses.

"Which is my room?" I ask, trying to put some enthusiasm into my voice.

Peggy smiles. "Let me show you around." She raises her arm, gesturing at four doors that lead off from the landing. "This first one is the bathroom and we've got a bath and a shower." She shuffles across the carpet, and I join her at the door as she pushes it open.

The bathroom isn't anything wonderful - a sink basin, a toilet, a bath with a glass screen covering half of it – but it looks clean enough. "Lovely," I say in response. "And you and Ron use this bathroom too?"

"We do," Peggy says. "But we get up very early, so we won't get in your way in the morning."

I smile in thanks. But I need to get up early, too, I want to say. Hopefully, it won't be an issue.

"Is that your bedroom through there?" I ask, pointing to the door on the connecting wall to the bathroom. It's an educated guess. That room looks out over the street and thinking about the footprint of the house would take up the lion's share of the upstairs space.

"That's right," Peggy says. "There's no reason for you to go in there so I won't show you."

"Of course. I get it." I turn around and waver between the two remaining doors. One is next to the bathroom, the other opposite this one, which means it looks out over the backyard. "And which is my room?"

"This will be your room." Peggy staggers over to the door opposite. The one furthest away from her room. That's a good thing. As I follow her over I get a better look at the other door and notice there's a metal bar-lock attached to the frame with a brass padlock.

I only realised I'd stopped to stare when Peggy turns back around and touches my arm. "You can't go in there," she says.

"Oh. No. Fair enough," I stutter. "Storage, is it?"

Peggy smiles. "That's Charlotte's room. We keep it locked while she's not at home."

"Ah, I see." But something about it doesn't feel right. Why a padlock? To me, it seems like overkill and not in keeping with the house's décor. A normal door lock, the sort I'm hoping is on the door to my room, would only cost a few pounds and look less like they had something to hide.

I brush these ideas away. It's those haywire instincts of mine trying to trip me up again. Plus, I'm tired and probably anxious about starting my course tomorrow. After a good night's sleep and now I know what to expect, I'm sure every-thing will look a lot different.

"Anyway, let me show you to your room," Peggy says, pulling at my arm. "It is so good to have you here, ducky. What joy. A young person staying in the house again. And one so lovely." She stops in front of the final door and looks up at me. "Is that your natural colour?"

I was about to say something else, but her question throws me off my train of thought. "Erm… Yes, actually. It is. Blonde by nature!"

I wince internally at this last comment. I don't even know what I mean by it. For a long time, I played the goof in an effort to make people like me. That's what my last therapist decided, at least. After she pointed that out, I vowed to stop doing it and these days I'm good at holding back, but it comes out sometimes when I'm tired. I need rest.

"It's such a lovely colour," Peggy coos. "It's very like our Charlotte's hair. She's natural too."

"Great. I thought so."

"Do you really think she looks like me?" Peggy asks, leaning forward.

"Yes. Definitely."

"I think she looks like you." Her eyes sparkle as she says this. It doesn't help my mood.

"Well, I'd say I'm lucky if I do look like her," I say.

But inside I'm screaming.

Please let me into my damn room!

Please just leave me alone!

Peggy giggles to herself and opens the door. A waft of stale air hits me in the face as I step through into the room and look around. It's bigger than I imagined, with a double bed to my left and a wardrobe and bureau against the opposite wall. A window with faded red curtains drawn across it faces the door and adjacent, on the wall, hangs an oval mirror that looks vintage and is probably worth something. Yet nothing in here is reminiscent of the photos I saw on the website.

Or is it? I can't remember.

I knew there was a double bed in the room and the other furniture looks familiar. It's the red curtains that have thrown me off but, like the wallpaper downstairs, there's no reason why they can't have changed these since the photos were uploaded to the website. On top of the bureau are a kettle and some tea and coffee-making facilities. There's even a small microwave unplugged on the floor beside the wardrobe. While I'm thinking about it, I take my phone out of my pocket to check the website. That way I can put my mind at rest. But as I pull it out, I see the battery is almost dead. Plus, with the bad reception here it's going to take me an age to connect to the site. If I can at all.

"Do you have wi-fi?" I ask, but Peggy looks confused at the question. "The internet?"

"Oh. Yes. We do. I like to go on it and get the weather and the news. Some of it is so hard to read though. Don't you think? They need to make the writing bigger."

I'm about to tell her there are ways around this, accessibility options, but I decide against it. I just want her out of my room so I can get into bed. I open up the wi-fi portal on my phone and scan the list of available networks. "Do you know which it is?" I ask, showing Peggy the screen.

"Hmm. Maybe that one?" she says pointing to one called *V3TT-Home.*

I click on it. "And the password?"

Peggy opens her mouth as if she's about to relay the information but then shuts it again. She frowns. "We did have one. It's written down somewhere. I'll see if I can find it for you."

"Brilliant, thanks." As I turn to face Peggy my eyes land on the door frame, and I see bolt locks, top and bottom. That makes me happier. "Is there a key for the room?"

Peggy looks flustered as if all these questions are some of the trickiest she's ever experienced. "Yes. I think so." She eases back the door and I see an old mortice lock with a key in the hole. "There we are. I thought so."

"Great."

I place my hands on my hips and wait. Thankfully Peggy gets the message.

"Well, I'll leave you to make yourself at home," she says, backing out of the room. "If there's anything you need, please just ask and—Oh? I almost forgot what would you like for breakfast?"

It's my turn to be flustered. I didn't expect breakfast to be part of the arrangement. In fact, I'm almost sure it isn't.

"They only booked the room for the five nights," I tell her. "I don't need you to cook for me." But Peggy looks down-trodden at this and even though my mood is growing more brittle by the second, I feel bad for her. I get the impression she misses her daughter. She probably lives for fussing over and mothering her guests. Maybe that's one reason why she opened up her spare room for visitors like me. Charlotte no doubt has her own life over in Liverpool and Ron doesn't strike me as being scintillating company. She's lonely. I know what that feels like.

"I need to make a quick getaway in the mornings," I add. "My course starts at nine-fifteen each day. It's only twenty-five minutes away by bus and there are two buses every hour, but I want to give myself an hour to get there, just in case. I wouldn't want you to have to get up on my account..." I trail off as I see the disappointment in Peggy's face. "But you know what? Tomorrow it would probably be a good idea to leave with some food inside of me. Just until I know what's available at the venue. So, thank you, that would be nice. A piece of toast and some coffee will be perfect."

"Do you like scrambled eggs?" Peggy asks, her voice brightening.

"Oh, I...Erm..."

"Yes! Perfect! I'll make scrambled eggs," she says, exiting the room. "Charlotte loves my scrambled eggs. And Ron does. I've not made them for a while."

With her back to me, I can't help but shake my head and smile at her as she leaves. She's a cute old lady – the sort of grandma figure you see in movies, like Nana Mary but not quite as stern - and I can't help but like her.

"Peggy?" I call after her. "Do you have the wi-fi password?"

She stops and looks back with a smile. "I'll find if for you."

"Great. Do you know when... that might be?"

She sniffs. "Tomorrow? Is that okay?"

I clear my throat. It looks as if it will have to be okay, doesn't it? "Yes. Thank you. Oh, and one more thing?" I suck air in through my teeth, aware I sound like a bit of a pain.

"Yes. What is it?" Peggy's face drops and for a split second it's as if a dark shadow has descended over her, but then she smiles and I wonder if I just imagined it.

"Do you have a key for the front door?" I say. "It's just - I'm not sure what time I'll be back from my course each day and I don't want to disturb you and Ron."

And it's kind of common practice if you're staying somewhere, I want to add. But I don't. She's a cute old lady and her mind is hazy at night time. It'll have slipped her mind. That's all.

"Didn't I give you one?" she asks, supporting my theory.

"No. You didn't"

"Well, not a problem. I'll make sure we get you one."

"Great." I raise my eyebrows at her, but it doesn't have the desired effect. "So… When?"

"Tomorrow," she says. "Don't worry, love. You have a nice rest. Good night. Sweet dreams."

And what else can I do? Despite the voice in the back of my mind telling me this is all a bit weird I wave her goodnight and close the door of my new room.

FIVE

I let out a sigh of relief as I close the door and lock it from the inside. It's been one hell of a long day. I fling my suitcase onto the bed and sit beside it, glad to be alone at last. I lay back and stretch my arms up over my head. The bed is firm but that's how I like it and the linen smells fresh. Lying here now I can't remember what was even bothering me about being here. I have my own room with a nice big comfortable bed and a door with a lock. Sure, the old couple who own the place may be a bit more involved than I expected, but I don't have anything to compare this to. I should stop overthinking it. After years of therapy, I'm aware that sometimes my mood can colour my experience of life. Fatigue and stress have an amazing ability to make an okay situation seem terrible - and make a welcoming landlady seem overbearing.

I sit up and stretch my neck left and right as I peer around the room. A framed print of an old ship negotiating stormy seas hangs on the wall. It looks ancient and isn't to my taste. But really, I have no idea what sort of art I do like. When you grow up the way I did you don't have the luxury or the time to consider such things. The painting is nice enough, I suppose. It goes with the room. I get up off the bed and go to the window, easing back the curtains. It's dark out and I can only see my reflection in the glass but when I put my face right up against it, I can make out a backyard and an alleyway intersecting this row of terraces and the one on the next street. The windowsill is free from dust which I appreciate and there is a porcelain figure of a female flamenco dancer on one side which is old-fashioned but nice enough. Despite Ron's obliviousness and Peggy's night-time haziness, it's clear from how clean the room is they were expecting me. If I get the chance tomorrow, I'll have another look at the listing on the VayCay Rooms website. I'm sure I'll see I'm worrying over nothing. And I've stayed in worse places over the years. Much worse. I puff out my cheeks as memories of dusty bedrooms with no furniture except for rickety cot beds, and scary dormitories with bunk beds crammed into every available space flash across my mind.

No. Don't get there.

That's all in the past. The future is all I care about now. It's all that matters. And that starts tomorrow when I begin my new journey as a HR professional. I close the curtains and return to the bed, unzipping my case and opening it out. My new laptop sits on top which I take out and place on the top of the bureau. Returning to my case, I'm not sure I've packed enough clothes, but I've certainly brought enough underwear with me. Why do we always do that when we go somewhere? I've talked about it with people and it's not just me. I can be going on a simple weekend away, but I take enough under-wear for an expedition to the North Pole. What am I scared of happening?

Buoyed by this silly thought I make short work of unpacking, hanging my three blouses in the wardrobe along with two jumpers, my navy trouser suit and three pairs of black trousers. 'Modern but tasteful office wear' is how I'd describe these outfit choices. They're all new items, bought when I first moved up to Manchester for my new job and with the last of the money I'd saved for such a venture. The job interviews with GP Telecom were all done over the internet, so I knew I'd already got the position whilst I was still in Oxford. Luckily for me, the landlord of the poky bedsit I was staying in was as dodgy as they come, so there was never a proper contract signed. With the offer of the new job, I was able to make the leap and move up north with some semblance of a safety net in place.

I also have my passport and an e-reader in my suitcase, but I leave them in the side compartment for now. I brought my passport in case I needed to show it to the hosts for ID, but I don't think Peggy is bothered. But I've often carried my passport with me. It's the way I roll. Or, rather, it was the way I rolled until I met Graham and he tricked me into thinking settling down in one place was the safe option.

Idiot.

So, I've got to make this work. I've got to prove to myself I can be the strong, resilient girl I used to be. Before he came along, convinced me to trust him and then ripped my heart out. What sort of prick does that to a person?

I put my suitcase in the bottom of the wardrobe and get changed into a pair of old leggings and an oversized black t-shirt with the words Nap Monster written across the chest. It was a stocking filler last Christmas from Graham.

A stocking filler.

Bloody hell.

I puff out another breath that has so much bitterness

behind it I can almost taste it. I feel stupid now to have allowed myself to grow content with, and reliant on, Graham's comfortable middle-class life. I never had stocking fillers growing up. I never had a stocking at Christmas, period. I remember getting a bar of chocolate one year, and another time an old Barbie knock-off, but her hair was matted and the plastic on her face and legs was scuffed and it was obviously second-hand.

I take my phone and lay on the bed with my head on the pillow. It smells fresh with a hint of lavender and I'm glad of its cushiony embrace.

"Everything is going to be fine," I whisper to myself. "You can do this, Lauren. It was meant to happen this way. This is the start of the next exciting phase of your life."

I've been saying something similar to myself for the past five weeks. It's become a bit of a mantra but I'm unsure whether it does any good. You see a lot of people on social media pushing the benefits of positive self-talk, but I always feel it's a con. Because you know, deep down, whether things are well or not. You can't lie to yourself. I know. I've tried.

Before I know what I'm doing I've opened up my phone and I'm scrolling through my photo roll. Most of the photos here are of me and him, or just him, or some expensive-looking plate of food from a restaurant he took me to. There are, of course, a few obligatory selfies – I've got a dark past but I'm still a twenty-eight-year-old – but most of the space is taken up with memories of him. I land on one photo from *that* night. The night Graham proposed to me. I'm sitting on his knee and holding my ring up to the camera with my mouth open wide in a goofy expression. I was ecstatic that night. It felt as if all the bad things that had ever happened to me had happened for a reason. That I was meant to go through all the shit so that

I could meet Graham and he could save me. I believed we'd be together forever.

What a damn fool.

That's the worst thing about being dumped four months before you're supposed to walk down the aisle. You don't only lose the man you loved but all your plans for the future.

I sniff and wipe the heel of my hand over my eyes. No. No tears. I promised myself I wouldn't do that. I've shed too many for that man over the last month. Yet, all at once I can sense the expanse of the universe all around me and how alone I am within it. I click off the photo roll and open my recent calls list. Graham's number is still on there, below Rochelle's - the head of HR at GP Telecom - and the taxi firm who took me to the bus station this morning.

My finger hovers over his number. It's almost 8.30 p.m. Even if he went to the gym after work he'll be back home by now. The urge to call him is so strong that I have to fling my phone on the floor to stop myself. As it clatters against the wall I panic and quickly jump off the bed to scoop it up. That was stupid and impulsive. I'm not like that anymore.

After checking the screen for damage, I can return to my position on the bed and open up WhatsApp. I don't know why I keep doing this to myself, but I go straight for his name and open up the long thread of messages that have accumulated over the last four years. Ever since he first approached me in that nightclub in London and asked for my number. I thought he was so arrogant that night but there was something about him too. He was tall and handsome and when he smiled at me it was as if fireworks went off inside of me. Whether that's what they call love at first sight I don't know, but it didn't take Graham long to say those three magic words once we got together. I took a bit longer, he used to try to coax them out of me, but I was scared to say it. Maybe a part of me knew he was playing a game, even then, But eventually, he got it out of me. I told him I loved him and I meant it. I loved him more than I thought I could ever love anyone. So much so that I moved with him to Oxford when he got his new job. I gave up everything for that man. The fact I had very little to give up in the first place is irrelevant. He picked me up, made me fall for him and then tossed me away when he was bored with me. I still don't have the full story from him as to why he called off the marriage - only that he 'couldn't do this anymore' - but whatever his reasons, it stinks if you ask me. I hate that bastard so much. The only problem is I still love him, too.

And I want to text him.

That's not so bad, is it? I'll keep it light, the same way I have done with the last few messages I've sent him since we split up. I read them back to myself now. Only one of them he's replied to – sending a laughing-face emoji and a single X to a joke I made about my new flat being smaller than our old kitchen. I remember when his reply arrived late at night two weeks ago. I agonised over that single 'X' for days. But he'd sent it at one in the morning. No doubt he was drunk and/or feeling horny. Regardless, I want to reach out to him. I can tell him about my course and that I'm staying in a weird house with a weird old couple. He'd find that funny I think and me doing the course shows I'm being proactive with my life. It shows him I don't need him. That I'm…

"Oh, bollocks."

With a groan, I place my phone on the small table next to the bed.

Don't be a loser, Lauren.

You're better than this.

A noise on the landing outside my room has me lift my

head off the pillow. I listen. It sounds like someone dragging something along the carpet. Then there is a voice. It's hard to make out what is being said but from the pitch and tone, I think it's Peggy. I hear her say something along the lines of 'This way you daft sod.' I smile to myself. It sounds as if she's helping Ron to bed. A warm feeling swells in my chest briefly, but it doesn't come to anything. I'm too tired and jaded for sentimentality but I do find it cute that they're still looking out for each other after all this time. I'd say they were lucky but I'm not sure that's the right word when you appreciate Ron doesn't seem to know who or where he is. I've also noticed a slight sadness behind Peggy's eyes whenever she talks about Charlotte. She lives in Liverpool they said but that's not that far away in the scheme of things. What is it, an hour on the train? My guess is she doesn't come back to visit as much as they'd like.

I hear the sound of a door opening and then closing and the voices grow even more muffled. That must be Peggy and Ron going to bed. I check my phone screen. It's only 8:45 p.m. That's good. If they turn in this early it means that, if I need to get a drink or use the bathroom, I won't disturb them. Or, more importantly, they won't disturb me. Despite the surreal-ness of being here in their spare room and it not being what I was expecting I don't mind it that much, but privacy is impor-tant. Not that I ever had much of it growing up. Or even when I was with Graham. He used to check my phone all the time and when we first moved in together, he made me give him my passwords. It was because he'd used my email address to get twenty percent off at some website and he needed to check the discount code he said, but I got the impression if I changed the password to something else, he'd be angry. So, I didn't. And yes, maybe that was a big red flag and maybe I'm better off without him but he was so kind and funny the rest of the time I sort of ignored those moments.

"Stop it," I whisper to myself. "He's gone. You're moving on."

Moving on up. Moving on out.

That's another of my recent mantras. But, like before, I don't really know what it means or if it helps in any way other than to fill my head with words instead of thoughts of Graham.

I get up, double checking my alarm is set for the morning and plug my phone in the socket near the door. I also check the door is locked and turn out the light. With my phone out of reach, I won't be tempted to use it if I can't sleep but I don't think I'm going to have any problems there. I've slept in so many weird houses over the years that one more isn't an issue. The room is almost pitch black as I move along the side of the bed, so I switch on the lamp on the bedside table while I get settled. The low-wattage bulb casts the room in a dim, eerie glow but even in this strange house, it doesn't bother me too much. I never feared the dark, even as a child. From an early age, I knew of real monsters in the world. Imaginary ones didn't get a look in.

Still, as I get under the covers and cast my eyes around the room, I feel a familiar flutter of trepidation in my stomach. With Ron and Peggy in their room, the house is quiet again. Too quiet. It feels as if my soul is absorbing all the silence and stillness around me. Normally that would tell me something was wrong but even if I was to trust my instincts – and right now I don't think I can – what other options do I have? Rochelle has booked this room for me and I have to accept it. I've no idea what the cancellation and refund policy is at VayCay Rooms, but I doubt they'd refund GP Telecom just because I found the accommodation a little off-putting. And right now, I can't personally afford to make alternative arrangements. But it's fine, I tell myself. I'm sure VayCay Rooms vet all the hosts they allow to advertise via their website. It would be in their best interests to have that as a policy, I tell myself, and the thought settles my nerves. I realise I haven't yet used the bathroom or brushed my teeth. Damn it. I wonder whether I should force myself, but I don't want to leave my room now I'm here. It's fine. I have an extremely strong bladder and will just brush my teeth extra thoroughly in the morning.

I prop myself up on my elbow and reach out to turn off the lamp. As I do, the light casts shadows across my arm, high-lighting the white mounds and hollows of the scar tissue I've carried with me for as long as I can remember. I hardly notice the scars now except for times like this when they're hard to ignore - a reminder of who I was and what has happened to me. I switch off the light and rest my head on the pillow. Forget vetting their host clients, if VayCay Rooms vetted the people who booked with them I might not have got a room anywhere.

SIX

My eyes snap open and I blink into the darkness for a few seconds, trying to work out where I am and why I'm awake. The creeping feeling of dread on the edge of my awareness doesn't help. Peering into the murky blackness I can make out dark shapes across the room and, to my left, a sliver of moonlight comes in through a crack in the curtains.

My course!

The spare room.

I reach out for my phone before remembering it's plugged in near the door. My fingers find the cold porcelain of the lamp stand instead and after grappling with the neck I switch it on. An orange glow fills the room and I glance around, wondering what woke me so abruptly. I hear no sound from the other side of the door but, as I listen further, I hear men's voices. They're coming from outside. Throwing back the covers I get out of bed and pad over to the window. The curtains are made of rough heavy material and creak as I ease one of them open a few centimetres. With only the lamp light I have a better view through the glass and, casting my gaze in the direction of the voices, I see two men standing in the backyard of the house two doors down. From this angle, I can't get a very good look at them, but I can see there are two of them and they're both wearing dark-coloured beanie hats. One of them has a beard and as I watch he leans down and picks up a hold-all before handing it to the other one. He says something in a low rumble. I can't make out the words, but the staccato rhythm of his speech makes me think he's giving instructions. I tense. I should stop spying on these dodgy men, but I can't stop myself. They've got to be up to no good. Why else would they be meeting up in a backyard in the middle of the night? And what's in that hold-all? The one with the beard places his hand on the other's shoulder and removes something from the inside of his jacket with the other hand. I can't see what it is, and I press my forehead against the window to get a better view. As I do I knock the flamenco dancer figurine over and it bangs against the glass.

Shit!

I grab the figurine and jump back as the man with the beard jerks his head in my direction.

Did he see me?

I'm not sure.

I count ten seconds and then lean forward to check. The backyard is now empty. Both men are nowhere to be seen. It doesn't help my increased heart rate. If they knew someone was watching them – someone in this house – that could be a problem. It could be dangerous.

Bloody hell, Lauren.

Why do I always get myself into messes like this? It was the same when I was younger and Julie, the mother of my second foster family, found me rifling through the filing cabinet in her office. I wasn't even interested in finding anything incriminating. I was only twelve. I was bored. And even now, it's not like I go looking for trouble. I'm a curious person, that's all. I always have been.

I wonder again about the VayCay Rooms vetting procedure. They wouldn't have accommodation on their site that was deemed unsafe, would they? But maybe they don't care? If they're anything like most companies I've dealt with they're as helpful and caring as can be until they get your money. Then you're on your own. There's probably a page of small print in their terms and conditions that absolves them from any blame in situations like this.

But what situation is this – really? I'm letting my imagination run away with me. It might have been some dodgy deal going on with those men just now, but if it was, it was more than likely a low-key thing. Cranbourne Street might need a little TLC but it's a quiet street in Market Allerton, not South-Central LA. That hold-all was probably full of duty-free cigarettes or stolen jewellery rather than anything too sinister.

I sit down on the bed and stare at the scars on my arms. I used to hate them when I was a teenager but now I don't mind them so much. They remind me of all I've gone through in my life, all I've endured. I'm a good person now. Or I try to be, at least. The welts and bumps are a road map of my journey to this point. And even if VayCay Rooms were to vet their customers, Peggy has nothing to worry about. What happened to me – what I did - was such a long time ago even I don't remember it. I'm not sure even if it shows up on background checks when applying for rental properties and the like. I have declared it, though, for the last two jobs I've interviewed for. I'd rather have it out in the open than worry it will come back and bite me on the arse if they do a more robust background check. This way I control the narrative, as they say. And, up to now, I'm glad to say no one has had an issue with it. There have been questions but I'm always happy to answer them and, on both occasions when I got the job, I think it helped my case. Indeed, good old Janet at Briars in Oxford - where I worked before the break-up - said she found my story 'incredibly inspiring'. I'm not so sure about that. It feels like a lifetime ago now. Then I met Graham and it was like none of my past mattered.

Until the day he told me it was over.

A shudder runs through me as if my body is trying to shake these thoughts away. I promised myself I'd be more optimistic from now on. Yet, sitting here in this strange house, with shadowy men doing nefarious deals outside my bedroom window, I feel more alone and vulnerable than I have done in years.

I get up off the bed and pick up my phone from over by the door. It's only 11:10 p.m. for heaven's sake! I thought I'd been asleep a lot longer than I have been. But the phone has enough charge now to last through to the morning and most of tomorrow. I unplug the charger cable and climb back into bed with it. I don't like screen time before sleep as it often keeps me awake but I need some connection right now. Or a distraction.

Snuggling down under the covers I swipe it open. But the signal is still as crappy as it was earlier. I open up Instagram, but it won't load. I try Facebook, same story. Even my emails take forever to refresh and, when they do, I'm presented with one solitary message - from a make-up company I bought something from a while ago offering me 5% off my next purchase.

Whoop-de-doo.

I check my alarm once more and am about to turn out the

lamp when I realise I'm still wearing my necklace. That's weird. I always take it off before bed due to the length of the chain being longer than the average chain. If I forget to take it off, I'll wake up with it all tangled up and it takes me forever to unravel it. The fact I forgot to remove it shows how worn out I was earlier. How worn out I still am.

I twist the chain around so the clasp is in front of me and unfasten it, before placing it next to my phone on the bedside table. It's silly but this necklace has become like a talisman for me over the years. I always feel safer if I can see it when I wake up, even if I'm not able to wear it. The fact that it belonged to *her* is rather ironic, but I've worn it for so long that it's lost all prior meaning and is now just a good luck charm for me. Or it's bad luck, depending on how you look at it.

The chain has broken twice in the past when I've forgotten to take it off, and I don't want to risk it breaking again and having to pay to get it fixed. Not now money is so tight. Graham did say he'd help me out with the deposit on my new place, and that he'd refund my half of the deposit we lost on the wedding venue. That's guilt for you, I guess. It shows the guy does have some feelings at least. But to date, I've had nothing from him. A laughing-face emoji and a single 'X'. That's all.

At times like this, when I'm alone with only my unhelpful thoughts for company I can't believe I let this happen to me. How could I have been so stupid? I've always been a plucky kind of girl - I've had to be with the life I've had - but at some point down the line that pluckiness turned into cockiness and I bought into the dream being sold to me. I actually believed things were going to work out the way I wanted. I had a wonderful man who seemed to love me with all his heart. He wanted to marry me and start a life with me. It was perfect.

But then four months before the wedding he takes me to the local pub after work and tells me it's over.

I shudder at the thought.

I can still see everything vividly in my mind's eye. I knew something was wrong from the look in his eyes, but I didn't want to articulate it to myself even for a second. I hadn't even taken a sip of my wine when he blurted out that he couldn't do this anymore. *This,* meaning what exactly? Marry me? Love me? Pretend he cared about me? It turns out it was all those things. And what an idiot I was. I should have known. People like me don't get happy endings.

But Graham took so much more from me than just my dreams of a happy life. My house was his house, all our friends were shared friends. Or so I thought. It soon became apparent they were his friends. He left me alone and unsure of who I was without him. That's what I hate most. He took my confidence. He took my pluckiness. Because of him, I'm unsettled and unsure of myself in most situations. I don't trust my instincts anymore. Somewhere between him sitting me down in that pub and his words ripping my heart out, I lost that part of myself.

And yet a part of me still loves him. A part of me knows if he was to call me and tell me he'd made a mistake I'd be so overjoyed I wouldn't know what to do with myself. That angers me as much as it upsets me.

My throat is dry. I throw off the sheets and climb out of bed, tiptoeing over to the door. I realise I must have some instincts remaining from my younger days, as I listen at the wood for a few seconds to make sure no one is outside before slowly twisting the handle and easing the door open. The landing is dark and I use the phone I'm still holding to illuminate my path across the carpet to the stairs.

Moving deliberately, in case a rogue creak or a groan from an old floorboard wakes Peggy or Ron, I descend the stairs down to the hallway. More photos in silver frames trace my path to the kitchen and I lift my phone to get a better look at a few of them. The theme here is the same as elsewhere in the house - there are a couple of photos of Peggy and Ron in their younger days; one of them on bikes on a country lane smiling sweetly at each other; another of them sitting at a banquet table with a large suckling pig laid out in front of them while Ron holds his arms out in mock-surprise – but most of the wall space is taken up by photos of Charlotte. I stop to take in a school portrait of her. In it she's about thirteen and is wearing a brace on her teeth. She looks happy and, with her blonde hair and a faint smattering of freckles, I guess I can see a slight resemblance between the two of us. But not enough to comment on.

There's something about all these photos of Charlotte in the house that I find odd, yet I can't put my finger on what it is. I frown as I cast my gaze back up the row of photo frames. Is it just that there are so many of her? If so, it's probably envy driving these ideas, rather than anything sinister. What I wouldn't give to have people who wanted to display pictures of me all over their walls.

I enter the kitchen but don't turn on the light. There are no blinds on the window and the moonlight provides enough light so I can see where everything is. Besides, if those men are still around, I don't want to alert them that I'm here. I go over to the sink in front of the window overlooking the backyard and listen. I can't hear anything, so I assume they're long gone. And it was also probably nothing untoward, just my stressed mind playing silly games with me. I take a glass down from the shelf next to the sink and get myself a glass of water from the tap, drinking half of it down in one gulp and filling it up again. The red glow of the digital clock on the oven to my right tells me it's 23:32. I should be asleep. I've got a busy day tomorrow.

Having quenched my thirst, I hurry down the hallway and am about to go back upstairs when something compels me to check the front door. It has two deadbolts at the top and bottom, yet they've not been bolted in place. Only a single Mortice lock guards us from the world outside. I tug on the handle to test it. It's locked. Good. I'm glad that even in her 'night-time haziness' Peggy remembers to lock the door. I'm trying not to judge the area the Cliftons live in, since I've stayed in much worse places - but it doesn't look safe with strange men hanging around late at night. But then I notice there's no key in the lock - or anywhere in sight. What if there was a fire? What if I had to get out in an emergency? An eerie feeling creeps up inside me as I realise that I'm locked inside this house for the night with no means of escape.

It's fine, I tell myself. The old couple upstairs no doubt feel vulnerable. They're protecting themselves and me. If I wanted to get out I could just go and ask them to unlock it. I take this as a good sign - and it's not like I've never been locked in before – but tomorrow I'll ask for my own key. Just to put my mind at ease. That's important and I don't think they can deny their guest's access. I might need one if the course finishes later than I expect tomorrow, or if I have a drink with some of the other attendees afterwards. The last thing I want is to turn up here when they've already gone to bed and have to bang on the door to wake them.

I yawn. There's no point stressing myself about this now. I have an early start in the morning and something tells me it's going to be another long day. I need to get some sleep. I take my glass of water up to my room and lock the door behind me. Once in the relative safety of my room, I vow to stop letting my imagination run haywire and to try to enjoy this time away. Yes, I was hoping to be staying somewhere more luxurious and less quirky, but this is the place GP Telecom has booked for me so I have to make it work. Still, before I climb into bed I double-check the bedroom door is locked and slide the deadbolts home as well. You can't be too careful.

SEVEN

I'm wide awake on the first beep of my alarm and after switching it off I leap out of bed and stretch. I slept a lot better than I thought I would in this house and with the new day comes a fresh wave of resolve. The past can go to hell. This is the first day of my new life. I'm going to complete this course; get the qualification I need and make a go of my life in Manchester.

Graham who?

I retrieve my towel and toilet bag from the wardrobe and unlock the door. The house is still and silent as I ease it open. Peggy and Ron must be still asleep. I walk across the landing towards the bathroom, passing Charlotte's room. It seems odd that it's locked up the way it is but if Charlotte knows her parents are letting out their spare room, she must feel safer securing her room so people can't enter. If most guests are like me - more curious than they should be – she's probably wise. The thing is, it's the very fact her room is padlocked that sparks the most curiosity in me. But each to their own. There were many times when I was growing up when I'd have longed to protect my space the way Charlotte has done. She's just being cautious. I get that.

I go into the bathroom. With the bright morning sunshine filtering through the frosted pane this room also feels different from the way it did last night. But whereas the new day brought with it possibility and hope just moments earlier, here it only seems to highlight the bathroom's shortcomings. It's not a horrible room, there's nothing about the basin and toilet units that are bad, but it's dated and worn and could do with what people call a deep clean. Black mould speckles the window frame and on the cracked sealant around the side of the bath. Exposed pipework runs down the wall and has been painted the same pale blue colour as the walls. I had hoped for more but it's what work has provided and if I want to go elsewhere, I'll have to pay for it out of my own money. That's not an option right now. I have a credit card but the last thing I need is to get into more debt when I'm trying to get my life back on track.

I place my toilet bag on the sink and pull out my toothbrush and toothpaste. As I go to work brushing my teeth, I examine my skin in the mirrored door of the wall unit. I might feel refreshed, but I don't look it. My eyes are puffy, the way they have been most mornings recently. I thought it was down to all the crying I'd been doing but I've not cried for a week now. I don't think I've got any tears left.

I spit out and rinse my mouth with water before undressing and stepping into the bathtub under the shower unit. There's a glass partition to stop the water from getting out but it feels loose as I grab it to steady myself.

"It's fine," I whisper to myself. I twist on the water and step back as ice-cold jets hit my chest. "It's only four more nights."

Plus, I'm going to be out for most of the day at my course and won't get back until late. By that point, I'll be too worn out to worry about anything other than going to bed. I stand shivering in the cold air as I wait for the water to get warmer. I was planning on washing my hair, but I can't be bothered. I have a canister of dry shampoo in my case. I can last a few days longer. Once the water is warm – not as hot as I'd like, but warm enough – I step under the shower unit and wash myself. As I do my mind drifts to Charlotte's room once again. I wonder what she's got in there that's so important she needs to keep people away. If she lives in Liverpool, why hasn't she taken everything of importance with her? Are there things in there she doesn't want people to see? Embarrassing things? Incriminating things? Videos? Photos? Maybe it's her mum and dad she doesn't want in her room, I wonder, as I switch off the shower and grab my towel to dry myself.

People have always told me I'm too nosey for my own good but when you've lived the life I have, it pays to be inquisitive. Curiosity might have killed the cat but when you grow up in the care system it can also save your life.

This aspect of my personality, coupled with my keen imagination, has me stop on the landing outside Charlotte's door on the way back to my room. The lock is made up of a piece of flat metal on a hinge that fits over a loop attached to the frame. An old padlock is hooked through the loop to keep the metal lock from opening but the screw fittings on both sides are loose and when I push against the door, I can open it a few centimetres. I gasp, glancing over my shoulder to check Peggy and Ron haven't suddenly appeared from their room. I'm only wearing a towel and I should really get back to my room and get dressed ready to leave. But I can't help myself. I lean closer and peer through the gap. I can't see too far into the room, but

I notice a sliver of pink curtain and, in the corner of the room adjacent to the door, four hold-alls are stacked one on top of the other. Beside these is a rickety old wardrobe that looks like it could fall to pieces if someone sneezed too close to it. I assume the bags are full of old clothes, stuff Charlotte packed up but didn't take with her when she left. I have two similar ones in my new flat I've yet to get around to unpacking. I lean into the door, pushing my luck as the old screws take the strain. But I can't see much else except for the carpet which is a horrible purple colour. Maybe that's the reason why they keep it locked.

"Is that you, dear?"

I jump and step back from the door, gripping my towel around me. It's Peggy but her voice is coming up from downstairs. I thought she was asleep in her room. I open my mouth, wondering how to reply when she calls again.

"Are you there?"

"Yes. Sorry. It's me," I call back. "I was having a shower."

"You found it okay then? The water takes a while to heat up sometimes."

I walk over to the handrail that runs around the top of the stairwell. "It was fine, all good."

"Do you want a cup of tea?" Peggy asks.

I wrinkle my nose. "Ah, no. Thank you. I really should get dressed and make a move."

"Oh, I see." She sounds hurt. I wait a moment, but she doesn't say anything else, so I hurry back to my room to get ready.

While I get dressed and apply a little make up my mind is on my course. Once I qualify, I'll have a diploma as an HR professional. It'll be the first decent qualification I've ever had. I never did too well in school but that was more to do with my situation and how many times I had to move around than my abilities. I think I'm clever enough so it shouldn't be too taxing. But I'm aware there is a certain amount of pressure on me. Work needs me to get this qualification, which means if I want to keep my new job I need to do well. It'll be fine, though, I'm going to work hard and put my all into it. Plus, it'll be good to have something else to focus on and take my mind off Graham and my personal troubles for a few days.

Once I'm ready I check myself in the oval mirror facing the door and then go downstairs. It's almost 7:30 a.m. and my plan now is to get to the bus stop and arrive at the venue with plenty of time to spare before the 9:15 a.m. start. In the course literature Rochelle sent over it said there was a cafeteria that served breakfast. I know I told Peggy I'd have breakfast here, but I'm sure she'll understand. I'd rather grab something to eat on-site, safe in the knowledge I'm there and ready for action.

As I get to the bottom of the stairs, I can hear the clink of crockery and the low drone of a radio coming from the kitchen. The front door is in front of me. Can I leave without saying anything to them? Would that be very bad of me? I've stayed in guest houses and Bed and Breakfasts before - and even some posh hotels after getting with Graham – but nowhere like this, where the owners are always around. I reach for the door handle, tensing my shoulders as I ease it open.

Bugger. It's still locked.

"There you are." My shoulders sag at the sound of Peggy's voice. "We're through here, love. In the kitchen. Come join us and have something to eat."

I lower my head for a second as I scan the area for the key, hoping I missed it last night. But it's nowhere to be seen. I really don't want to be late on the first day, but Peggy sounds so insistent. She's a nice old lady and maybe it's just that she reminds me of Nana Mary, but I don't want to upset her. Besides, there's still something bothering me about Charlotte and the locked room upstairs. I'm sure there's an entirely innocent and rational explanation for the extensive security measures but I'd like to know what it is. Maybe over breakfast, I'll learn more about Peggy and Ron's enigmatic golden child and why she's so scared of people seeing in her room. With this in mind, I turn around and head for the kitchen.

EIGHT

"Is it okay if I just have a slice of toast?" I say as I enter the kitchen. "I really do have to get off pretty soon. Also, are you able to unlock the front door for me because I couldn't see the—"

"Ah you'll have something more substantial than toast," Peggy interrupts. "You can't go out for the day on an empty stomach."

"No honestly. Toast is fine. And I really do need to get moving. I have to be somewhere at eight," I lie.

Peggy's face drops. "I've got some eggs here," she says. "I thought you might like some. Charlotte loves my scrambled eggs. Doesn't she, Ron?"

Ron, who is sitting and staring at the salt and pepper mills in the centre of the table, makes a grumbling noise. "Aye. She loves them."

I smile at him and then back at Peggy. My jaw aches I'm smiling so much. The clock on the oven reads 7:35. If I leave here by eight that will still give me ample time to get to the venue before the course starts.

"Okay, thank you. Scrambled eggs would be lovely."

I sit down in the chair offered by Peggy and she goes to work cracking eggs into a bowl and whisking them with a fork.

"What is it Charlotte does?" I ask. I already know the answer, but an awkward air has descended on the room and it's the first question that comes to mind.

Ron clears his throat as if he's going to respond but before he has a chance Peggy turns around. "She's a nurse," she says. "She's a good one, too. Isn't she Ron?"

He nods. "Aye. She's a good girl. She works hard. Always has done."

"Does she come back to visit you much?" I ask, immediately regretting this as Peggy's eye twitches and she looks away.

"Not as much as we'd like," she says, shifting her attention to the bowl of eggs. "She moved to Liverpool to study nursing and loved the city so much she stayed there. I don't blame her. Who wants to live with their parents when they're thirty-four years old? But we do miss her."

"Oh? She's thirty-four?" I ask.

Peggy nods. "Yes. That's right. She was born on the eighteenth of August nineteen eighty-nine. I can remember that day like it was yesterday. I wish it was yesterday."

I narrow my eyes and look at Ron. I could have sworn he told me last night that Charlotte was the same age as me, twenty-eight. But then, I don't expect Ron to be the best source of information these days, poor old sod. It also makes more sense if she's thirty-four. I'm usually good at guessing people's ages and I'd say Peggy was in her late seventies. That means she was in her early forties when she got pregnant but that's not unheard of. If Charlotte was a last-chance baby and they'd been trying for one for many years, it also explains why they dote on her so much.

"Has Charlotte left a lot of expensive things in her room?" I ask as Peggy tips the beaten egg mixture into a frying pan already spitting with oil.

She looks over at me with a confused expression. "What do you mean?"

I grimace. I know I'm being forward and sound cheeky asking this, but I can't shake my curiosity. "It's just with the padlock on the door, I wondered if she had valuables in there. I don't blame her for having a lock, to be honest. I was wondering, that's all. Sorry, I am rather nosey I know."

Peggy throws Ron a look, but it's not reciprocated. "There's nothing up there much now. A bed, for when she stops over, and a few personal things. Our Charlotte is a very private person, that's all. She took most of her stuff when she left for Liverpool, but she still comes back all the time to visit. She might pop over while you're here, actually. I hope that's okay with you. You'd like her. You look a bit like her you know..." She frowns. "Sorry, love. What's your name again? It's slipped my mind."

"No worries," I say. "It's Lauren."

"Of course. I don't know what's going on with my memory at the moment. I think it must be the cold weather." She rolls her eyes and I glance out the window at the grey skies. "Now what were we doing?"

"The eggs," I say, pointing to the sizzling pan behind her.

"Oh yes of course." She spins around and busies herself getting a plate out of the cupboard and tipping the scrambled eggs onto it. I watch her, as a slight slinking feeling descends over me.

Poor Peggy's night-time haziness seems to have extended

through into the morning. Should she be hosting guests if she's becoming so forgetful? I assume she's been caring for Ron all this time but what happens to couples when they both become too vulnerable to look after themselves? Does Charlotte know what her parents are like these days?

If she's as amazing as these two make out and visits them regularly, why hasn't she noticed something is wrong? Why is she letting them do this? I appreciate they might need the extra cash that letting out their spare room provides, but if they aren't up to the task... I let the thought go as Peggy places the plate of eggs in front of me.

"Delicious," I say. "They look great."

They don't. It's more like an overcooked omelette than scrambled eggs and half of them are burnt, but I smile and make the appropriate noises as I chew them down.

Peggy sits opposite me and watches as I eat. It's quite off-putting and the whole time I'm trying to think of something to say to ease the discomfort.

"How long have you been renting your spare room out?" I ask.

She blows her cheeks out as if it's been so long she can barely remember. "Charlotte will know," she says. "It was her idea, wasn't it Ron?"

Ron mutters something under his breath that I don't catch so I just nod and smile and hope it's the right response. I decide I'm going to stop asking about Charlotte and the room. I'm not getting any kind of answer and I'm already sick of hearing about her. I know I sound bitchy – and I've done enough work on myself to know it's probably my own issues driving these feelings – but I can't help it. I suppose I wish I had someone who cared about me and talked about me as much as Peggy and Ron do about Charlotte. I hope that woman appreciates her parents.

But they are her responsibility, I remind myself.

They're not mine.

Even though I want to - and try to, sometimes - I can't save every broken soul I come across. That was something Graham and I used to always fight about. I think it annoyed him how I always rooted for the underdog. He'd often scold me for giving money to homeless people or getting involved in situations that didn't concern me when I felt someone was being wronged. But when you grow up the way I did you get a real understanding of what it's like to be down on your luck. I hate to see people suffering.

As I swallow down the last of the eggs, I get a real hankering for a mug of tea or coffee, but Peggy hasn't offered me a drink since I sat down and I don't have time now to wait while she fusses around. I'll grab one on the way, or at the venue.

"Right, I really do need to get going," I say, standing. "Thank you for breakfast, that was above and beyond. I'll make sure I leave you a good review on the website."

Peggy smiles up at me the way some old people do when they have no idea what you're talking about.

"You're a good girl," she says.

"Oh, while I remember," I say. "Is there a key for the front door that I can have? I don't know what time I'll be home tonight, and I don't want to disturb you if it's late. Obviously, I'll lock up after myself and make sure the door is secure."

"Did we not give you a key?" Peggy asks, looking at Ron and then back at me.

"No. Not yet."

"Gosh, I am sorry, duck. We'll sort one out for you, won't

we, Ron?"

Ron grunts. "We've got keys. Loads of keys. I think there's one in the bedroom I can get you."

I stand in the doorway and wait but neither of them moves.

O—kay.

"So…can I have a key?" I ask, giggling as I do to cover the awkwardness. "As I say, I might need it for later."

"We'll be home, don't worry," Peggy says with a smile so sweet it seems almost false.

"Right. Yes. It's just…" I sigh. "Never mind."

What's going on here?

Do they not want me to have a key?

"Ron will find you the spare one if you need one," Peggy adds. "But we don't go out much these days."

Yes, I get that, I want to tell her. But I also don't like being locked in a house I've no way of getting out of. It happened to me a few times growing up and I'd really prefer not to continue that trend into adulthood. Especially not when the only reason I'm here is to help create a new life for myself.

"A key would be good though if you don't mind."

"We don't mind at all," Peggy says. I'm about to leave but as I turn, I see her expression drop and for a split second I detect a hint of something else behind her eyes. I wouldn't say it was malice exactly, but it's not far off.

I pause in the doorway.

Have I said something wrong?

Should I ask her what it was? Should I apologise?

But then she sits back and beams a wide smile at me and I realise I must have I've imagined it. She's a nice old lady and I'm anxious about my course. Not to mention the fact I'm still overthinking every single occurrence because I no longer trust my instincts after Graham messed my head up so monumentally. I need to get a grip. I need to calm down. I glance at the clock on the oven. I also need to leave for the bus.

"Eek, I'm going to be late for my bus. I'll see you tonight," I say and begin to walk down the hallway. I get all the way to the door before I realise the damn thing is still locked.

Bloody hell…

Turning around I'm about to storm back in the kitchen when I'm startled by Peggy standing behind me.

"Whoa! Shit!" How the hell did she get there so quickly and without me hearing her?

"Oh dear," she whispers, holding up a large brass key. "We don't need that sort of language, do we?"

"No. Sorry. I didn't mean to…" I trail off as she reaches around the side of me and places the key in the lock. "Thank you. Sorry. I'm just a bit stressed."

Peggy scrunches up her nose at me. "Have a good day," she says, pulling open the door.

A cool breeze encircles us. I give her a nod of thanks and step outside. What a lot of bother over a bloody key, I think as I glance both ways down the street. But, in the long run, who cares? It might even be fun staying here. It'll be a good story to tell people if nothing else. Maybe even male people on dates if I ever reach that point again.

As I'm walking away towards the bus stop, I hear the key turning in the lock behind me. For a moment it gives me cause for concern but then I laugh it off. Something is seriously odd about that house but it's nothing I can't handle, and Peggy and Ron seem nice enough if not a little forgetful. If my experiences up to this point have taught me anything it's that you've got to make the best of what you're given in this life.

Four more nights.

What's the worst that can happen?

NINE

I've already researched the bus timetable and know there are two buses every hour – one at twenty minutes past and one at twenty minutes to - that will take me to the main entrance of Samstone Manor. The HR course starts at 9:15 a.m. and the journey takes twenty-three minutes according to Google maps. It means, after my unexpected delay back at the house, I'm cutting it fine time-wise and will only have a few minutes to find the room where the first module is taking place. My morning coffee will have to wait until the first break but that's fine. This is a new adventure and I'm prepared to roll with the punches when I need to. I've been doing this all my life but, after Graham, I feel it's doubly important to focus on the positives. This is a new start for me.

The first day of the rest of my life.

And no matter how cliched that might sound it spurs me on as I hurry down the zigzagging backstreets of Market Allerton towards the bus stop. The area still looks drab and run down even in the daylight which I think is a bad sign for an area. Despite the cold weather, the sun is out, and I always think most places look nice in the sunshine. Most places. Not Market Allerton. It might have been a pleasant little town once, but most of the shops on the high street are now boarded up and their facades covered in grime and dirt from exhaust fumes.

I reach the bus stop with a few minutes to spare and use the extra time to compose myself. Two other people are already waiting here: a man in a grey suit about my age and an older lady wearing a thick black tube coat that looks about three sizes too big for her. I turn away and flatten my hair, casting a surreptitious eye at my reflection in the window of the betting shop next to the bus stop. I don't look as bad as I imagined I would. My hair is a little fly away after not washing it and it will need a cut in a few weeks, but I look presentable enough and as I smile at myself my confidence grows. That is until I turn back and catch the eye of the man in the suit.

He's smiling but it's clear he's been watching me, and I detect humour in the way his mouth twists up at one side. Is he laughing at me because I was checking myself out just now? Is he mocking me?

No. Stop that.

You're being paranoid again.

That's not what we do.

Instead, I smile back but in a clipped sort of way. Polite, not flirtatious. Hell, I'm not sure I'd even know how to be flirtatious these days. Although, I can't help but notice he is rather good-looking. Good looking for a man waiting for a bus in a run-down town, at least. He's tall, about the same height as Graham and with broad shoulders that hint at the fact he works out. His hair and eyes are both dark brown. In fact, it's his eyes that I notice the most. They say the eyes are the windows to the soul and his hint at compassion and intelligence. But then, that's what I thought about Graham's eyes.

I look away. I wish I could stop thinking about that bastard ex of mine. Before I know what I'm doing I've taken my phone out of my pocket and am tapping out a message to him. I tell him about the course and that I'm enjoying being in Manchester. I tell him about the weird accommodation, but that work has booked it for me, so I can't really complain. I keep the tone of the message light and jovial and try to make a few jokes. I'm happy with it right until the point I hit send and see the grey balloon turn blue. Then my heart drops into my stomach and I want to cry.

What an idiot! What will he think of that message? And what am I expecting to happen? The best I can hope for is another bloody laughing face emoji. If I'm lucky. Annoyed at myself I place the phone back in my pocket and look up to see the man is still staring at me.

Okay, that's a bit creepy now, mate.

Eyes forward and all that.

Something inside of me makes me gawp back at him and as I do, he nods his head as if in recognition and says, "Morning."

"Morning," I mumble back.

I look away and am glad to see the bus appear around the corner at the end of the street. Saved, by the X82 from Loggerheads to Shrewsbury. I straighten my back and wait for my turn as it pulls up in front of us. The older lady in the tube coat gets on first but then the man in the suit steps aside and waves me on before him.

"It's fine," I stammer, but he's insistent.

"Go on. After you." He seems friendly enough. His eyes

sparkle in the early morning sun as he gestures for me to board.

"Thank you," I tell him before clambering aboard.

It's been a while since I travelled by bus, but it seems the same set-up as usual. I pay the driver for a return fare and stuff my ticket inside my phone cover before turning away to find a seat. It's a single-decker bus and I'm dismayed to see most of the bench seats are occupied. I walk down the aisle, peering left and right in the hope I've missed one. All the other passengers stare straight ahead and avoid eye contact. One woman has taken up the seat next to her with four shopping bags that are straining at the seams with groceries. It's unfair that she's doing that, but I can't really blame her. As I walk further down the aisle, I see there's one free double seat left, in front of the raised rear seating area.

Yes! That one's mine.

But as I sit down and make myself comfortable my heart sinks. The man in the suit is making a beeline for the seat beside me. He grins greedily as he gets closer.

"Am I okay to sit there?"

"Yes. Sure." I shuffle up against the side of the carriage to give him as much room as possible. A second later the bus shudders and pulls away from the stop and we're on our way.

Twenty-three minutes and counting. Then I'll be there, starting my course, my new adventure, carving out the new and improved Lauren Williams. I close my eyes and take some deep conscious breaths as I tell myself how lucky I am for this opportunity. I've worked hard on myself every day of my life since I got out of the care system and I deserve some success and happiness.

This is a good thing. I tell myself.

Everything happens for a reason.

But I also know it's not always possible to force yourself into a proactive mindset so when I open my eyes and don't feel any different, I'm not too surprised. Disappointed, maybe, but not surprised. I take out my phone to check if by some miracle Graham has replied, but he hasn't. The fact I can see the message has been delivered and read sends a deeper wobble of disappointment running through me but I look out the window to distract myself.

After a few minutes, we leave the town behind, and the dirty shop fronts and grubby streets become trees and open fields. Suddenly life seems a lot more hopeful. I can sense the man beside me is looking at me as if he wants to say something, and I can't help but glance his way.

"Lovely day, isn't it?" he says, gesturing out the window with a flick of his eyebrows.

"Mmm. Yes." I look away and feel my cheeks flush.

Come on, Lauren.

Pull yourself together.

"Sorry, I don't mean to be a pain," the man adds, perhaps picking up on my frostiness. "Who wants some stranger talking to them this early in the morning? And about the weather. Dear me. It's just, I'm new to the area and don't really know anyone."

I feel myself relax slightly. This guy might be a tad over-friendly, but he seems to understand social norms enough to not be a creep.

"I'm afraid you're out of luck there," I tell him. "I'm only staying in the area for a few days."

"Ah. That is a shame. I mean… I've bothered you for nothing." He seems embarrassed. "I'm Pete, by the way."

I smile. "Lauren."

"Pleased to meet you, Lauren. So, you're visiting friends or...?"

"I'm here on work," I say, helping him out. "Do you know Samstone Manor? I'm attending a five-day course there this week. But the venue's accommodation was full so I'm staying at a guest house in Market Allerton. Well, someone's spare room, actually. My work booked it for me. But it's decent enough."

He scrunches up his face. "Sounds like you've got a busy week. What's the course?"

"Becoming an HR Professional," I say. "I've just got a new job and they want me to complete the qualification before I start in the role. So, the pressure is on me a bit." I laugh and so does he and I sense myself relaxing some more. "I'm sure it'll be fine. You say you're new to the area?"

"That's right. I've got a new job too. At a security firm over in Shrewsbury. I'm in tech support. I won't bore you with the details but it's not a bad place to work. I moved here last month. It's a bit of a fresh start for me. I split up with my girl-friend six months ago and wanted a clean break."

I look away out the window.

Wow, Pete.

I see your six months and raise you six weeks.

"Sorry, you didn't need to know that," he says.

"No. It's fine. It's not that," I tell him. "It's just a bit close to home for me, that's all." I laugh again but I don't sound convincing and I'm aware I've cast a veil of awkwardness over the scene. "Whereabouts do you live?" I ask him.

"Cranbourne Street. Not too far from the bus stop. A five-minute walk."

"Ah, cool. That's where I'm staying," I say. "At number forty-seven."

Pete leans back and looks at me as if I've just told him I'm his long-lost sister. "No way. I'm at fifty-one."

"It's a small world." But as I say this, an image of the two shadowy men from last night flashes across my mind. I don't know which direction the houses are numbered on the street but if they go right to left as I'm looking at Peggy's house then number fifty-one is the one where the men were. I glance at Pete up and down. I remember one of them had a beard, but I didn't get a good look at the other one.

Shit.

My breath catches in my throat as a thought hits me.

Did he see me watching him through the window last night? Has he approached me today to work out whether I saw something I shouldn't?

I quickly brush these ideas away. I'm being paranoid. Pete seems like a nice man and it's not helpful to speculate. A lot of people have strong opinions about me when they discover who I am and where I come from without ever knowing the real me. I never want to be like them.

"Is it a nice place?"

Pete's question snaps me out of my head. "Sorry?"

"Where you're staying. Is it nice?"

I chew on the inside of my cheek as I consider how to answer. I don't want to insult him if he's recently moved to the same street.

"It's good enough for what I need," I say. "To be honest when I heard I'd have to stay over I did hope the company might put me up somewhere more lavish, but hey ho. It's only for a few nights."

"Ah, yeah. I get what you mean. It's not the nicest of areas, is it? I don't think I'll stay here long once I get on my feet again. I'm only renting, thankfully."

I nod. I'm not sure what else to say on the matter.

"Are the people nice who you're staying with?"

I can't help but laugh at the question but stop myself in case it turns into hysterics. "They're okay," I say. "Peggy and Ron are their names. They're old and a bit senile, I think, but pleasant enough. I keep wondering if there's been some kind of mix-up with my booking, but I don't want to rock the boat with work."

"A mix-up? How?"

I shrug. "The house looks different from the photos I saw online. But it's probably me misremembering. It's not a big deal." Although it might start to be, I think to myself, if Peggy doesn't get me that key and continues to fuss around me.

Perhaps this shows on my face because Pete frowns and his smile turns into one of sympathy.

"Well, it's nice to meet you, Lauren. I hope your course goes well." I'm about to respond when he points out the window. "I think this is you."

As the bus slows to a stop, I follow his finger and see a large stone entrance set back beneath some trees. High walls on either side run parallel to the roadside and the words Samstone Manor are carved into a stone archway that spans the open gates.

"Shit. Yes. Sorry. Can I…"

I jump up and Pete does the same to allow me to shuffle out into the aisle. "I'm getting off here," I shout to the driver, pressing the button for the bell as I go.

The driver opens the doors and I thank him and jump off onto the pavement. A teenage boy gets on after me so I've time to hurry across the road and reach the entrance of Samstone Manor before the bus sets off on its travels. As it does, I turn back, ready to give Pete a wave of thanks. He's shifted across into my old seat and is staring at me out of the window. I raise my hand at him and smile but he doesn't respond. Or, rather, he does, but it's not what I was expecting. His brow is furrowed and the way he's looking at me makes me feel uneasy. As the bus moves away I lower my hand and hurry through the entrance of the manor. I can't worry about this now. I've got a qualification to get.

TEN

I have no time to locate the cafeteria and grab a coffee before the course starts. In fact, I'm barely through the main doors and giving my name and company details to the woman at reception, when an older lady with grey hair pinned up on her head ushers me down a long corridor towards the main lecture hall where inductions are already taking place.

As I reach the lecture hall I'm presented with a room full of people, all milling around and with a low hum of excited conversation in the air. Thankfully I don't seem to be as late as the grey-haired woman implied, but after arriving with only minutes to spare – and coupled with the fact I'm not staying on-site like the rest of them - I feel instantly out on a limb. The other attendees are mostly women, around my age or younger and have already divided themselves up into seven or eight smaller groups. I watch them as they chat and laugh together as if they're old friends. A lot of them are sipping large cups of coffee which makes me doubly jealous. I wander over to the nearest group to try to ingratiate myself into the throng.

"Hi there, sorry, is this the right place for the CIPD HR professionals' course?" I ask a dark-skinned girl with the shiniest hair I've ever seen.

I chose her because she was the first to make eye contact with me, but she looks me up and down as if I'd torn her away from hearing the punchline to the greatest joke of the century. "Yes, that's right," she says.

"Great. Thanks," I say, nodding and smiling to keep her engaged. "Are you staying at the manor?"

"Yes. We all are, I think."

"Oh, I'm not. I was booked on the course late, so the sleeping quarters were full up, unfortunately. But I've got a nice little place in the next town. I'm Lauren, by the way."

The woman purses her lips at me "Marsha," she says, swaying her shoulders as if to demonstrate how desperate she is to return to the group. Before she gets the chance the static crackle of a microphone pierces the air and we all look towards the front of the room where a tall blonde woman has appeared.

"Good morning, everybody - and how are we all this fine day," she says, doing a good impression of a presenter on a light-entertainment television show. "My name's Carol and I'm one of the main facilitators on this course. I'll also be presenting the module on coaching and mentoring in the workplace tomorrow which I think will be a lot of fun for all of us. So, welcome to Samstone Manor and the HR Professionals course. It's great to have you here."

She holds her hands up as if awaiting a response and a low murmur of thanks rumbles around the room.

After the introductions we're told to get into pairs and that we'll be doing some 'getting to know you' exercises for the first part of the morning. My heart sinks when I hear this. Especially when the attendees quickly get into twosomes and

I'm left on my own, spinning around on the spot like a confused ballerina as I search for a partner. I spot another lone soul across the other side of the room.

"Do you have a partner?" I ask as I march over to her.

Up close I'd say she was in her early thirties. She's smaller than me and seems nervous as she introduces herself as Katherine, with a K. I get the impression she's an outsider here too and that's fine by me. Carol informs us we are to have a short chat - to introduce ourselves and to tell our partner who we are and what we want to achieve this week. Then we're to disclose a secret about ourselves.

I *hate* stuff like this. I might have purposefully constructed a personality for myself over the years that is both sociable and affable, but I'm a rather shy person when it comes down to it. Besides I'm worried Katherine with a K might run a mile if I was to tell her some of my deepest darkest secrets.

Where to start? I could tell her my biological father was a petty criminal who used to beat my mum up before he landed himself in prison after a botched robbery. I could tell her my mum was a drug addict who got *really* into the smack when I was about four years old and that when I was naughty she'd stub cigarettes out on my young flesh. Or how about the big one – that at the age of seven, I'd clearly had enough of her and ended up pushing her down the stairs where she broke her neck and died. I bet none of the other attendees here is sharing secrets like that one. It's a real doozy and no mistake.

I don't say any of this to Katherine with a K, of course. She would probably have a heart attack. Instead, I tell her that even though I don't have kids I sometimes watch children's TV shows as I find them relaxing. This is sort of true, I don't actually watch much television at all but I have been known to watch Bluey or Peppa Pig on occasion. You'd be surprised how good they are. There are plenty of jokes in them that adults can appreciate and I'm safe from any triggers that might send me spiralling. Although that hasn't happened for a long time now.

After my mum died – because that's the way I've always looked at it, she *died* I didn't kill her – I had loads of tests and assessments done on me to make sure I wasn't some demon child. I was never informed of an official diagnosis but they must have decided that what I did was due to circumstance, rather than me being a cold-blooded killer. Even to this day, I'm not sure exactly what it says on my record regarding what happened, but it has shown up on some of the more vigorous background checks that have been carried out. I had to have a special interview when I was applying for my passport, for instance.

Being in care is mostly all I remember of my childhood. I was passed around from care home to care home for many years. I started in Ealing, West London where I was born, and ended up in Croydon via Bexley and Leatherhead. Fostering was an option, but most families didn't want me after finding out what I'd done. There were two that did try fostering me, but I was hard work back then and they weren't able to cope. Not that I was a bad kid, for most of my childhood I was as nervy as Katherine with a K, but over the years I learned to stick up for myself. At first, it was with my fists and feet but later I learnt to use charm to make the other kids like me. I got by. But then, as I got older still, I began to feel guilty and hated myself for what had happened. I believed it was my fault that I was in this situation. I'd see other kids in the street with their parents and wish it was me in their place. I spent so many years wishing my life away, dreaming I was someone else, or that I was somewhere else. I think that's why I developed such an overactive imagination. Being that way, living in a fantasy world, was the only way I could survive.

But there were snippets of happiness to be found in and amongst the grimness of the care system. Nana Mary was one of them. She ran the home in Leatherhead where I lived from the age of ten to thirteen. She was lovely and really treasured all the kids in her charge. With me being at such an impressionable age I found solace in a lot of her words. She taught me a lot about the world and how I needed to be to get along. I still say it's because of her influence I was able to thrive once I turned eighteen and was sent out into the world to fend for myself. I imagine Mary was only in her early seventies back then but to the pre-teen me she seemed ancient.

Back at Samstone Manor - and after Katherine has revealed her secret love for the singer Michael Bolton - we move onto the next task. This time we're asked to spend half an hour on our own and to fill in a personality test. I take my paper over to the side of the room and flick through the first few pages. Carol says the results will come in useful for later modules in the course and, despite having misgivings about how accurate these sorts of tests can be, I fill it in as truthfully as I can. We also get a chance to grab a drink at this point in the proceedings and I'm very grateful for the complimentary tea and coffee which is located at the back of the room. I make myself a large cup of coffee with two sachets of instant and three servings of milk, all topped up with hot water from the industrial-sized urn in the corner. It tastes pretty bad, but the caffeine is needed, and I take it back to my desk feeling alert and ready for what's next.

Once everyone has finished the test, we mark them up and I discover I'm a Blue - which means I'm an omnivert, whatever that means, and somewhat of a people pleaser.

Hmm. Tell me something I don't know.

Maybe there's something in these tests after all.

I've heard it called that before – being a people pleaser – and I don't like that phrase, but it's no surprise to me. They say victims of childhood trauma go one of two ways: either they trust no one and can become sociopaths, or they ache to be close to other people and will do whatever it takes to achieve love and acceptance. I'd like to think I'm not so weak-willed these days, but that's because I've worked on myself enough and am aware of my issues. I don't let people walk all over me.

Most of the time, at least.

Graham was a different matter.

After leaving care, I struggled for a few years but then with the help of my social worker, Gareth, I managed to get a job for a company that sold sanitary products to hotels and service stations. I was office-based, taking calls mainly and it was only temp work at first, but the boss liked me and after six months they offered me a permanent position. I enjoyed the work and it felt good to be busy but it was the structure and the social aspects of the job which helped me grow most of all as a person. I loved answering calls and practising my 'office voice' as I called it, and the other girls really helped me appreciate who I was and what I could offer the world. It sounds a bit silly, perhaps, but that job was the making of me. Then, a few years after that I met Graham and my life seemed to finally fall into place. With each day that went by the darker parts of my past faded away. I felt myself softening as I gave myself to love. I was happy. I was content. And I never thought either of those things could be possible.

But maybe I was right all along.

This is why I don't trust anyone anymore. Least of all

myself. It's why I feel vulnerable and rather nihilistic about life right now. I'm sure it'll pass. I hope it will. But it's also the reason why I'm here. And why I'm putting myself through this week. I've got to learn how to make life work on my own. It's scary as hell, but I can do it.

I have to.

ELEVEN

Despite the morning sessions being a real drag, the afternoon ones practically fly by. There is so much information to take in I can hardly keep up. But I suppose that's what comes from cramming a terms-worth of work into a five-day fast-track course. I am, however, glad to be out of my head and focusing on something other than Graham.

The module we're working on is entitled *Understanding Organisations and the Role of Human Resources* and the subject matter is as dry as it sounds but no less intense. There are hundreds of slides and note-taking to be done on topics such as *STEEPLE* analysis and something called the *Cultural Web*. I'm to choose one of these models and complete a mock analysis for my place of work as homework this evening.

I didn't know there was going to be homework as well!

I suppose it will give me an excuse to hide away in my room when I get back to the house. I like Peggy but I was hoping this week might provide space and time for quiet reflection as well as my getting a qualification. I could do without all the fussing around.

We manage to fit one more module in before the end of the day. This one is on how to develop ourselves as 'Learning and Development Practitioners'. The subject is interesting but by this point, I'm flagging and as I glance around the room, I see a lot of the other attendees look like I feel. The tutor for this module is the grey-haired woman from this morning, who introduces herself as Dr Janet Halliwell. Her delivery style is as terse and abrupt as her greeting was this morning. At one point, I catch the eye of Marsha with the good hair and smile and roll my eyes at her, but she snaps her attention away without even a smile in return.

Fine. Be like that.

I look around for Katherine with a K, who is sitting facing me but on the next table. I offer her the same sympathetic smile and this time I get a nervous grin in return.

That'll do. Thanks, Katherine.

It does feel a bit like school and we're a group of bored kids messing around behind the teachers' back, but I find comfort there for some reason. For a brief moment, I feel a part of the group. I never liked going to school when I was younger, but that was because I never settled in any one place. Plus, I had the stigma of everyone knowing I was a care kid. I think I would have liked it – and would have probably done well - if my circumstances were different. But, hell, you can say that about so many things.

Dr Halliwell also sets us an assignment for this module. We're to summarise her lecture in a self-assessment report on ourselves and our own development and then create a document of ongoing reflections that we should add to for the entirety of the course. I did hope the course might involve more reflection and less work if I'm honest. As I say, I never really tried very hard at school so exams sort of passed me by mostly. I'm not used to so much pressure in such a short period of time. Indeed, by the end of the afternoon sessions, I have a throbbing headache and feel nauseous. There are five more modules to be done over the next four days and some of them sound like fun. Hopefully, they'll rely more on practical-based learning than homework.

By the time Carol re-appears and thanks us all for our hard work today it's already gone 5:30 p.m. The buses back to Market Allerton only run every hour, on the half-hour, so I'll have to wait around until 6:30 p.m. for the next one. But that's fine. As the room breaks up for the day most of the attendees hang around but drift into small groups once again. After a full day, they seem even more cliquey and impenetrable to me than they did this morning. I slip my laptop into my bag and move over to the side of the room, scanning the groups for a friendly face, a way for me to ease into a conversation. Marsha with the good hair has her back to me over on the far side of the room but I don't consider her an option any longer and Katherine with a K is nowhere to be seen. I imagine she scurried away to her room as soon as the last module was over to complete her assignments.

With nothing else to do and feeling more awkward and alone than I've felt in a long time I head for the nearest table and take out my laptop and the stack of handouts from today out of my bag. I might as well do my homework now.

Let's hear it for Lauren, the teacher's pet.

It doesn't take me long to complete the STEEPLE analysis for my current role. Mainly because I haven't started there yet so I have free rein to make most of it up. It's a way of assessing how different external factors - social, technological, economic, environmental, political, legal and ethical - can affect a business. I write a paragraph or two on each section and I'm not sure if I do a good job, but it's done and out of the way. I'm hoping this is one of those courses where you can't really fail as long as you do all the work and show willingness.

Once I've finished and have written half a page for Dr Halliwell on my development over the last five years and what I want to get out of the course, the muscles in my hands are going into spasms from all the typing. I don't think I've typed this much in such a short time in my whole life. I sit back and read through what I've written, feeling like I'm one of the brainy, conscientious girls who always got good marks and praise from the teachers when I was at school. A lot of the kids like me – the ones from care or broken homes - would tease these sorts of girls and even bully some of them, but I was always jealous of their resolve and drive. They're probably all heads of companies by now, making serious money.

I pull my phone out of my pocket and see it's time for me to catch the bus. In fact, despite having an hour to kill earlier, I'm now going to be late if I don't get a move on. I don't want to wait around another hour for the next bus. I overhear one of the other attendees saying they're 'all going to the bar for a drink before dinner' and it makes me feel even more alone and unpopular. I can't be certain of it too, but I catch one of them giving me a funny look as they walk past. It's as if I'm the ghost at their feast. An unwanted addition to their fun. I know what that feels like because it's how I've felt for a lot of my life. But no more, I tell myself. I am a strong person. I can do this thing called life.

Gathering up my laptop and papers I stuff them into my bag and then make my way out. As I rush down the final section of the corridor to the main entrance, I'm half-expecting

Dr Janet Halliwell to be standing there, ready to scold me for running. But the foyer is empty. I head for the large double doors and push through to the outside.

The air is cool and it feels more wintery than ever as I stride on through Samstone Manor's ornate gardens. Tall, rich evergreens line the gravel path that snakes through the estate and maybe if I had more time, I'd stop to appreciate the scene, but today it's just a blur of green as I hurry through and join the path that takes me back to the roadside.

I check my phone as I get to the bus stop and am relieved to see I've got a few minutes to spare. I exhale a long breath, catching myself before I spiral out of control and instructing myself to calm down. Today has been a whirlwind. I've not had a chance to think about anything other than analysis models and personal development plans and my head is throbbing. I know this qualification will help me in the long run, but I wish it was a little less intense and a little more fun. With everything that's been going on for me recently, I've almost forgotten what it feels like to be carefree and have fun. I yearn to be silly, to laugh, to throw caution to the wind. I glance back at the manor, imagining all the other attendees having a great old time as they quaff glasses of pinot grigio.

Bitches.

The thought is in my head before I can stop it and I tell myself off immediately for thinking that way. That's the old me talking and I know how unhealthy it is to hold grudges or hate people for having what you want. But don't I deserve a little fun - a little pampering - after all I've been through? All I want right now is my own space, and to have a long soak in a hot bath.

I picture the spare room back at Peggy and Ron's house

and then the cold bathroom with its faded blue walls and exposed pipework.

It makes me sad.

But maybe this is all I'm good for. Maybe wicked girls from care homes don't get to live a nice life or stay in luxury hotels. Those things are for other people. Normal people.

I realise I'm spiralling again and roll back my shoulders to reset myself. I know from years of experience when I get caught up in thinking this way, it's destructive and futile. I'm doing all right for myself given the circumstances. Yes, I'd rather be going anywhere else right now than back to Peggy's spare room. But I can do this. I'm strong.

I straighten up to my full height as the bus appears further down the road. It's bang on time and as it gets closer, I step forward and put my hand out to show the driver I'm waiting. As it comes to a stop and the motorised bi-fold doors ease open, I step up into the cab and wave my return ticket at the driver. He doesn't look at it, or me, but sniffs and jerks his head down the bus, indicating for me to take a seat.

Shit.

As I turn and head down the aisle my heart drops into my stomach. Pete is sitting halfway down the bus on the right. I freeze, wondering if I can jump out of sight. But he's already seen me and waves me over.

Damn it.

This is the last thing I need.

With the course so intense, I've not had a chance to think about Pete all day, but now, here in front of me, a wave of dark thoughts and troubling concerns fills my mind. Was he one of those men in the backyard last night? And if so, did he see me watching him? And if both of those things are true - is he going to hurt me?

I'm not sure these are questions I can ask him – or even want to know the answer to - but as I glance around, I realise the space next to him is the only free seat.

So, like it or not, it looks like I'm going to have to talk to him.

TWELVE

I had been counting on it being a quiet journey back to the house. I'd even planned on spending the time doing some breathing exercises. The technique I use was shown to me by a therapist some years ago but I never felt the need to practise it until Graham broke up with me and my world was once more turned upside down. It would have helped settle my nerves after such a hectic day, but as I peer down the packed bus I know any sense of calm will have to wait.

As Pete continues to wave, I throw my attention down the bus hoping to see a free seat up at the back. But they're all occupied. Down to my right, a young couple are sitting together on one seat with their three children together in front of them. The kids are only small, and I wonder if I could squeeze on the edge of their seat, or even ask them to give up their places. They are only kids after all. Yet, they look like a sweet family and I'd hate to be the sort of person who'd kick up a fuss over something so trivial. I'm still considering my options as the bus sets off, making me lurch forward. I grab one of the upright steel poles next to the driver's cab to stop myself from falling into the aisle and making a complete tit of myself. Once I'm steady, I look up and see Pete is now standing up and beckoning me over. *All right, mate. Calm down.*

I can't ignore you now, can I?

Feeling my cheeks burning, I stride down the bus.

"Hey, again," he says, sitting and shuffling up so I can sit beside him.

"Yes. Fancy seeing you here."

"Sit down. Please." He smiles.

I twist my mouth to one side as if I'm going to refuse, but what would be the reason?

I'd rather not if that's all the same with you, Pete. I've had a real stinker of a day and part of me is worried you're a dangerous drug dealer.

No. I can't say anything. So, I sit, perching my buttocks on the furthermost edge of the seat before realising this is a pointless exercise and adjusting myself into a more comfortable position.

"How was your course?" Pete asks.

"It was good," I say. "A lot more work than I expected but I enjoyed it."

"Excellent. So, you're not going to lie low for the rest of the week and just tell your work you completed the course?"

I laugh. "I wish. It's a proper qualification that I need for my new job. If I don't get it there's no job."

"Oh, wow. I see. Sorry to sound flippant."

"It's fine."

"I suppose it's a lot more pleasant for you being in a nice old stately home than hanging around the delights of Market Allerton."

"Delights?" I smile. "Are there any?"

He frowns comically. "I'm not sure. There are a couple of awful pubs, as well as a few I'm too scared to go into. And don't forget all the charity and betting shops. Where did you say you were from again?"

"I don't think I did. I've just moved up to Manchester but I lived in Oxford before that."

"There you go then," he says. "Market Allerton versus Oxford. There's no contest."

I laugh and he looks at me like I've offended him before laughing along with me.

Ah, shoot.

As we talk, I'm more convinced than ever that he's a good guy. My instincts aren't what they were, and I don't trust myself to spot red flags the way I used to, but no one is this good an actor. Especially not shadowy men who exchange packages with other shadowy men late at night. I feel ridiculous for even thinking Pete might have ulterior motives. But I have to be sure.

I twist around in my seat, so I've got a better look at him. "Can I ask you a question?"

"Erm. Okay. Go on."

"Do you own a dark-coloured beanie hat?"

He splutters. "I wasn't expecting you to ask that!" He frowns. "I don't think so. I'm not a hat kind of guy. Why? Do you think I should get one? Have you noticed a bald spot?" His hand goes to his crown, and he looks hurt.

"No. You're fine. You've got a good head of hair as far as I can see."

"Phew. Thank God."

I chew on my lip. "You said you lived at fifty-one, yes? So, is that on the left or right of where I'm staying? If I've got my back to the road."

He frowns again. "it's on the right. Near the post box at the end of the street."

"Great. Yes. I thought so."

"Why do you ask?"

"No reason. I was wondering, that's all." I smile at him, feeling my cheeks burning again. This time it doesn't bother me so much. In fact, it feels sort of nice.

For the rest of the journey we chat and joke together and I sense myself easing into Pete's company. He's easy to talk to and it's been a while since I've had the chance to converse with anyone in a way that's not heavy with subtext and emotion. I even find myself talking about the break-up and it isn't weird or embarrassing.

"It must have been awful for you?" Pete says after I've relayed to him a summary of what's happened to me this last year. "It's hard enough breaking up with someone, I know how that feels. But to lose your home as well. That's rough."

He looks at me with such pity in his eyes that I can't bear it and have to look away. But it's true. When Graham told me it was over, he took more than just my heart. My home was his home. My friends were his friends. I lost everything.

"It is rough," I say, once I've swallowed back any troubling emotions that might set me off crying. "Or, rather, it *was* rough. I'm getting there. Day by day."

Pete smiles. "That's the spirit. I think that's all you can do. Take it one day at a time. You seem like a good person, Lauren. You should be proud of yourself for making a new start the way you have. Not many people would have your determination."

I laugh at this. I don't know why. I'm about to tell him determination is sometimes all I have but before I have the chance he sits upright and leans across me to ring the bell.

"We need to get off," he says.

Once we've disembarked, we stand at the side of the road and I watch the bus as it makes its way further up the road. It's almost seven and still light but the sun has set and the sky is an eerie shade of blue-grey.

"Listen, I don't suppose you fancy a drink, do you?"

I look at Pete, surprised at his question. But I'm even more surprised at how excited I am with the prospect of continuing our chat over a drink.

"I'm not sure," I say, trying to play it down. "It's getting late and I don't have a key to the house yet. I don't want to get back too late and have to disturb my hosts."

Pete nods. "Sure. I get it. We can at least walk back together and continue our—"

"But one drink won't hurt," I butt in. All of a sudden the idea of going back to Peggy's house fills me with dread. "And I do need to eat something."

"Great," Pete says. "There's a pub around the corner that serves food. I've not eaten there so I'm not sure of the quality."

"Is it one of the awful pubs or one of the ones you're scared to go into?" I ask.

He grins. "One of the awful ones."

"Well, that's sold it for me," I tell him. "Why don't you lead the way."

THIRTEEN

Pete wasn't kidding about the awfulness of the pub. The Golden Fleece is a five-minute walk from the bus stop and, as we walk in, I'm immediately hit by a musky smell of stale beer. It's one of those big, purpose-built pubs owned by a corporate brewery with a large bar area opposite the entrance and a smattering of round tables in the vast space in between. The carpet is threadbare in places, sticky in others. Wooden booths line the perimeter of the space and to the right of the bar is another smaller room that seems to be laid out for dining. The regulars all turn and look us up and down with fixed sneers as we make our way to the bar.

"Are you sure you want to eat here?" Pete asks.

Not really, is the short answer. But my only other option is to grab a day-old sandwich from the local off licence and eat it in my room back at the house. I peer at the chalkboard next to the bar on which is written a selection of 'daily specials.' I see they have fish and chips. That will do. You can't go too wrong with a deep-fat fryer and frozen produce.

"It doesn't look too bad and I am hungry," I say.

Pete smiles. "Why don't you grab a seat in the back room, and I'll get us some drinks."

"Are you sure?"

"Of course. And I'll bring a menu through as well. What are you drinking?"

"I'll have a pinot grigio if they've got it."

"No worries. A large?" I widen my eyes at him and nod eagerly and he laughs. "Coming up."

"Can you order me a fish and chips as well," I ask him. "I don't need a menu."

He gives me a thumbs up and an approving smile and I walk through into the smaller room feeling rather pleased with myself for some reason. I needed this. It's the first bit of light relief I've had for a while, and Pete is good company. He's funny, smart and not too shabby in the looks department if I'm honest. The fact I'm thinking this way buoys me up even more. Only two weeks ago I was telling myself I'd never look at another man for as long as I lived. I don't for one moment think anything will happen between Pete and me – I'm only here for a few days, after all – but it does feel good to be in his company. It feels even better to not have to go straight back to the house.

A surge of nervousness swells in my chest as I think of that place and I wonder, should I contact Peggy and let her know I'm going to be late? If this was proper accommodation, I shouldn't have to do that. I wouldn't have to do it now if I had a bloody key for the front door. I'm not leaving tomorrow morning until Peggy provides me with one.

"Here we are, a large pinot." Pete appears beside me holding my glass of wine and a pint of pale lager. He sits opposite and places the drinks on the table. "Oh, and here's your order number."

He slides a slip of paper over to me and I pick it up to see my order of fish and chips. at the bottom. It shows the price and that it was paid for with cash. "Pete, I didn't mean you should pay for it! I would have given you the money."

Or, at least, I would have put it on my credit card.

"Forget it," he says with a wave of his hand. "It's my treat. They'll call your number when it's ready."

"Are you not eating?"

"I'll get something later. I might pinch one or two of your chips though." He flashes his eyes at me.

"You bloody won't!" I say and he laughs. Then I laugh. It's nice.

We continue in this fashion for the next hour. Pete is fun to be with and has an excellent way of looking at the world and relationships. So much so, that I don't feel weird talking to him about Graham or his ex – who was called Fiona and sounds like she was a total bitch towards the end. I feel myself relaxing so much I don't even feel self-conscious when my food arrives, and I have to eat in front of him. He does steal a couple of chips, but I let him. It's the least I can do. Although I do bite the bullet and get another round of drinks in for the two of us using my credit card. I shouldn't, really, but after the first wine my resolve is down, and it only makes me want another one.

"I really have to get back after these," I tell him as I return to the table with the drinks. "Poor Peggy will be worried about me!" I say it like I'm joking but inside I'm concerned about what I might find when I get back to the house.

"She sounds to be a bit of a character," Pete says. "But I don't envy you having to stay there. I'm not sure I could deal with feeling beholden to the host the entire time."

"I know what you mean. And when work told me they

were booking my accommodation I was hoping for some-where a bit more lavish. A proper bed and breakfast place, at least. I don't quite know what happened. But my new work sorted out the room for me and I don't want to rock the boat with them. The last thing I want is to be labelled a pain or to be seen as ungrateful before I even start in the role."

"Yeah, tricky one," Pete says. He sits back and his face turns serious. "But they're nice enough people? The Cliftons, is it?"

"Yes. Peggy and Ron. You've not met them?"

He shakes his head. "I've seen her when she's been hanging out her washing on the line, but they keep themselves to themselves as far as I can tell."

A thought comes to me and I lean forward. "Have you ever seen their daughter, Charlotte?"

He narrows his eyes. "They've got a daughter?"

"Yes, apparently, she lives in Liverpool but comes back to visit. Her room is still there for her when she does. But get this - they've put a padlock on the outside of the door. It's a bit odd, don't you think?"

Pete sways his head from side to side. "Maybe. They might just be being cautious. You southerners, coming up here with your fancy ways, eating our fish and chips, they've got to be careful."

I smile at his attempt at humour, but it riles me a little that he's not taking my plight seriously. But then, maybe I'm the one who's taking it too seriously.

Lauren Williams? Overthinking things?

Surely not!

"Do you have any photos of inside the house?" It's another surprising question from Pete and as I blink in response, maybe he realises this too. "Sorry. All I mean is, I'm really into seventies and eighties décor," he adds, sipping at his pint.

"O-kay."

What's going on here?

I lean back, trying to ignore the voice in my head.

"I know it sounds like I'm being a nosey neighbour," he adds. "But I'm not. Well, maybe I am. But from what you said, the Cliftons haven't decorated for some time. I just love old interiors and would love to see some of it if you have any photos."

I fold my arms. He doesn't look the type to be into retro design, but who am I to say what he should be interested in?

"I think I've still got the email from work with a link to the listing. Let me check." I slide my phone out of my pocket. "I was going to have a look yesterday, but the signal was terrible."

"Yeah, it can be a bugger around here. That's country life for you."

I swipe open my phone and go to my emails. It's a new account I made recently and I find the one from Rochelle Green at GP Telecom without any fuss. Pete leans over the table and I tilt the phone for him to see as I click on the link in her email which takes me to the VayCay Rooms site.

"Oh. That's strange."

The page that opens is an error page – a 404 page I think they call it. The code for a broken link.

"Is it not working?" Pete asks.

"Doesn't seem to be. But it was. I was looking at it on the bus journey down here."

Pete leans back. "Never mind. Maybe they take the listing down if someone is renting out the room?"

It's a possibility but that doesn't sound right to me.

Wouldn't they want it to remain on the site so people could book alternative dates?

"I don't suppose you heard anything weird last night, coming from the back of the houses?" I ask as the thought hits me. "It was around eleven."

Pete sticks out his bottom lip and shakes his head. "I don't remember. Weird in what way."

I sigh. Should I say this? Does it make me sound pathetic? Like an anxious idiot?

"I saw two men in the backyard of the house two doors down," I blurt out. "It looked like they were doing some sort of deal. One of them was giving the other a hold-all. It was at number forty-three, I think. I'm not certain what they were up to, but it looked dodgy to me."

"I see. But you think it could be drugs?"

I tense my shoulders. "I don't know. Sorry, I shouldn't have said anything. I don't want to give you a bad impression of the area if you've just moved here."

"No, it's fine. I mean, I have just moved here, but I don't know how long I'll be staying in the area." He lowers his voice. "Did you get a good look at either of the men? Or what was in the hold-all? Did you see any money change hands?"

I shrug, realising the wheels have come off this story of mine rather quickly. "I didn't get a good look at either of them. Sorry, I shouldn't have said anything." I push my wine glass away and get to my feet.

"What's going on?" Pete asks, furrowing his brow. "Have I said something wrong?"

"No. It's me if anything." I let out a strange sound which I think is supposed to be a self-deprecating laugh. "It's just my stupid imagination running riot again. I'm going to use the bathroom. Can you watch my things?"

"Sure." He stares into my eyes and his lips spreads into a crooked half-smile that makes me feel slightly light-headed. I blame the wine.

Turning before I fall further under his spell, I wander across the room and through into the main area. As I go, I can't help but imagine Pete watching me walk away and pulling an approving face. The thought has me giggling like a silly teenager.

It's definitely the wine.

It has to be.

Please tell me I haven't become one of those women who get all giddy at the first sign of male attention. If so, this break-up has messed me up more than I realised.

When I get back from the bathroom Pete is gazing out the window with his pint glass poised at his lips, looking deep in thought. I also notice my phone screen is lit up and get a rush of excitement.

Is it Graham?

Has he replied to my message?

With the alcohol lowering my defences, the thoughts take over and I scoop up my phone to check. But there are no new messages. There are no new notifications at all. My phone must have been still illuminated from when I was checking my emails. What a rotten tease it is. And what a fool I am to think I could get over that prick so easily. He's still got me. I'm trapped.

"Lauren, is everything okay?"

I look at Pete. I wish it was. But all at once I feel stupid and embarrassed and like I don't want to be here.

"Do you want another drink?" he asks, getting to his feet.

"No, I— Shoot, is that the time?" I lift up my phone to show him the screen. "I need to get back to the house. Peggy and Ron go to bed around this time, and I don't have a key." I gather up my things.

"Can I walk you back?" Pete says, lifting his jacket off the back of his seat.

"No, it's fine. Really. You stay and get yourself another drink. I need to go."

He grimaces and rocks from foot to foot. "Are you sure? I don't want you to walk back to the house alone. Like we've agreed, Market Allerton isn't the nicest of places."

"Seriously, don't worry about me," I tell him. "It's still relatively early and I can handle myself. Thank you for dinner and for the drinks. I'll see you later. I have to leave."

Before he can respond I turn on my heels and hurry out of the pub.

Damn it, Lauren.

You were having fun for the first time in months.

But all I can think about as I speed-walk down the street towards the house is that I hope I'm not too late. I'm not sure if last night was a one-off but if the Cliftons are already asleep in bed, they might not hear me knocking. I'd expect Peggy at least to stay up until I returned but she said herself she gets hazy the later it gets in the day. I can't count on the fact she's even remembered I'm staying there. If she's locked up and gone to bed, then I'm screwed.

FOURTEEN

All the lights at the front of the house are off as I turn the corner at the end of the road. A panic fills me and I quicken my pace, running the last thirty yards down Cranbourne Street and pushing through the gate. When I get up to the front door I see through the dappled pain of glass in the centre that the kitchen light is on. This gives me hope as I ring the doorbell. I listen for a moment and press it again when I can't hear any movement. Then I knock on the door. I can hear voices drifting over from the next street along. It doesn't help.

Come on Peggy, please be up.

I try the door handle, but it's locked. I bang again, louder, using the heel of my fist. Putting my face up to the glass I call out. "Hello. It's me. It's Lauren."

A minute goes by, maybe two, although it feels longer. I keep banging my fist on the door with increasing force until, finally, I see movement in the hallway beyond.

Thank God.

"Hey, it's me. Sorry. Can I come in?"

I see a shadowy form, distorted by the dappled glass. As whoever it is gets closer, I stand up straight and, as the door is unlocked, put on a sheepish smile. The door opens a few inches to reveal half of Peggy's face. She squints at me.

"Who is it?"

I swallow. "It's me, Lauren. Remember? I'm staying here for a few nights."

She glances over her shoulder and then back at me and it's as if her memory has been rebooted because her face lights up. She opens the door wider and beckons me inside. "Come in, ducky. What are you doing standing out there in the cold?"

Well, the bloody door was locked and I don't have a key, I want to yell, but I just grin and splutter something about it being fine now.

"I am sorry I'm so late," I add. "The course went on longer than I expected."

Peggy shuts the door behind me and I'm about to pursue my 'can I have a key' enquiry when I hear a scraping noise coming from the back of the house. I also notice a draft in the hallway that remains when the front door closes. It makes a change from the oppressive heat from the radiators but seems at odds with what I've come to expect.

"Is everything all right?" I ask as Peggy moves past me.

"Yes, dear. We're grand. Have you eaten?"

"I have, thanks I—" I frown, tilting my head as I hear another noise coming from the kitchen. It sounds like something heavy is being dragged along the lino. "Is someone there?"

Peggy smiles. "It's just my Ron getting a bit of fresh air. He sometimes gets a bit hot and needs to cool down. Especially at night-time."

Yes, I don't blame him.

"Fair enough," I say.

"We've never managed to coordinate our temperatures in all the time we've been married." She chuckles and rolls her eyes, and I can't help but laugh as well. Doing so allows me to step back from my anxiety enough to calm down. I'm here, I'm safe. I had nothing to worry about.

"We were about to turn in for the night," Peggy says. "I thought you'd be back before now."

"Yes. I know. Me too. But that's why I need a key for the front door. Did you manage to get me one?"

"Yes. Of course. I'm not sure where I've placed it, but I'll find it for you in the morning."

I force a smile. I really would appreciate having the key in my hand but, ever the damned people pleaser, I don't want to appear ungrateful.

"Thank you," I say. "As long as I have it before I leave. It's another early start for me tomorrow so I'm going to go straight up to bed. I'll just get a glass of water first if I may."

I try to move around Peggy to get to the kitchen, but she doesn't budge. "I've put some water in your room." She says it in such a triumphant manner I stop and look at her. "That's right. I've put two big bottles up there. We usually have them for guests. I'm sorry they weren't there for when you arrived."

"Oh. I see. Great." I bite my lip, suddenly feeling very self-conscious. The two large glasses of wine have hit me more than I realised. "I suppose I'll go up then."

"Goodnight, dear. Sweet dreams." Peggy remains staring at me. Neither of us moves.

"Yes. You too."

Something feels wrong here, but I can't quite put my finger on what it is. I reason it's my semi-inebriated state that's causing me to feel this way. The wine, coupled with the fact

I'm exhausted physically and mentally. It's not only Peggy who sufferers from night-time haziness around here.

I climb the stairs and head into my room, locking the door behind me. True to her word Peggy has placed two litre bottles of mineral water next to the kettle on top of the bureau. I grab one and unscrew the top, gulping down half of it in one go. It'll hopefully negate any hangover that might be on its way. I take one last gulp, swilling the water it around my mouth and gargling before swallowing. I should clean my teeth and wash my face, but I can't be bothered. I do, however, manage to get undressed down to my knickers and pull on an old t-shirt before climbing into bed. The sheets are cool and the pillow is soft. It encases my head as I lay down and I close my eyes, already sensing sleep's benign embrace. Darkness. Oblivious-ness. It's been a long day. It's going to be another long day tomorrow. I sense a swirling mass of doubts and questions forming on the edge of my awareness but for now, I ignore them.

I'm too tired to worry.

Too sleepy to care.

What seems like seconds - but could be hours - later I'm pulled from unconsciousness into the dreamy world of half-sleep. I don't open my eyes, but I'm awake. I know who I am and where I am. A brief internal scan tells me I don't need the bathroom and I'm not going to be sick. Has something else woken me? I make a quick decision not to think about it and allow myself to sink back into oblivion until…

What is that?

Did I fall back asleep?

It's not initially clear to me if I'm awake or dreaming but as my awareness spreads, I'm certain I can hear a noise. It sounds like footsteps outside my room, then hushed voices, so quiet they're almost imperceptible. Was it this that woke me? Or is this still a dream? I still don't open my eyes. The bed is so warm and cosy, like a cocoon. I feel safe here. The duvet and pillow feel as if they're a part of me. I don't want to wake up properly. The door is locked, I tell myself. I'm fine. Everything is rosy. What I'm hearing is simply Peggy coming to bed, or maybe her helping Ron to the bathroom. It's cool. It's all cool. Sleep washes over me once more. A blessed release from my imagination. Nothing matters…

Shit!

That was most definitely a noise!

My eyes snap open and I blink into the gloom, my senses now alert for whatever has woken me. When you grow up in care you learn to sleep in environments that are both scary and unsettling but that doesn't mean I don't get scared.

And there it is again.

I lift my head off the pillow to listen. A soft scratching noise is coming from the other side of my door. I tense, unsure of what to do as my mind races to the dark corners of my imagination. My head is cloudy and I'm not able to focus my thoughts on any one thing. Why the hell did I drink two large glasses of wine?

I hear the scratching noise again. It's only faint but it sounds like nails scraping on wood. Or claws. My breath quickens and I sit upright in bed. There is definitely someone, or something, on the other side of my door. I grab my phone off the bedside table and swipe open the screen. The time shows it's 2:24 a.m. So, I have been asleep.

"Hello?" I say, but my voice is wobbly and hardly there at all. "Who's there?"

There's no response but the scratching stops. I throw back the covers and walk over to the door, checking the locks are all in place before pressing my ear against the wood. I can hear something. It sounds like heavy breathing. Or panting.

Or is that just me?

Could it be a dog or a cat? I haven't seen any sign of pets and no one's mentioned any, but that doesn't rule out the possibility. Cats are often out of the house most of the time. And they are nocturnal. Maybe this is where it normally sleeps and…

No!

The scratching goes again. And from my position behind the door, I can tell it's coming from too high up to be an animal. This realisation sends a fresh shiver of fear running down my body.

"Who's there?"

Nothing.

"Peggy, is that you?"

The scratching stops. I listen at the door but can't hear anything else.

What the hell?

I wait another thirty seconds or maybe longer and tiptoe back to bed. I'm under the covers for all of a minute when the crushing realisation dawns on me that I need to pee. That is not what I need right now. I roll over and try to ignore the sensation but the pressure in my bladder is too strong.

Why did I drink two glasses of wine *and* a litre of water before bed?

Aware of how fast my heart is beating, I throw off the covers and switch the light on, scanning the room for something I can take with me to use as a weapon if needed. I know I'm being ridiculous, but it will make me feel safer on my trip to the bathroom. I pick up the flamenco dancer figurine from the windowsill but it feels flimsy, so I put it back. A glass vase sits on top of the chest of drawers opposite. The neck is slim enough to handle and leads down to a heavy base. I reckon it could do some damage in the right circumstances. I pick it up and feel the weight of it in my grip. It'll do. It'll have to.

I walk over to the door and listen. I can't hear anything. No panting. No scratching.

Did I imagine it?

Was it all just part of a dream?

I step back. "Is anyone there?"

When no one responds I ease open the dead bolts and unlock the door. Then, raising the vase over my shoulder I grab the door handle and open the door.

"Oh! Shit!" I scream and jump back in fright.

Ron is standing in the doorway. He makes a weird yelping sound and pulls his hands up to cover his face.

"Bloody hell, Ron!" My arm holding the vase shakes with tension. I lower it. "What are you doing?"

He peers at me from behind his hands. Up to this point, I've viewed him as a weak old man and a rather doleful soul. But standing here in such proximity he strikes an imposing figure. He's hunched over and wiry but still a foot taller than me. His lined, jowly features distort into a wet-lipped smile.

"Charlotte, you're awake," he mutters. "I was waiting for you."

I flinch as he reaches out and strokes my hair and yelp as one of his fingers touches my cheek. It feels rough and cold. I shove his hand away. "Ron. Please don't do that." This is too freaky for me.

"Charlotte? What ever's wrong, my darling?"

"I'm not...I'm... Ron, I think you're a bit confused." I look past him across the landing. The door to his and Peggy's room is open.

Where the bloody hell is Peggy?

He steps forward, trying to get into my room. I hold a hand up to him, fingers tightening on the vase in my other hand. "Ron, no. This is my room. I'm staying here, remember? I'm not Charlotte. I'm not your daughter." He pushes against me. He's stronger than he looks and more determined. "Ron! Please! Peggy!"

"I only want to see you."

"Peggy!" I call out. "Help me!"

I have to lean against him to physically stop him from coming into the room. This isn't right. I've lived in some strange places and put up with some not-very-nice situations over the years, but nothing like this.

"You've got to leave," I tell him through gritted teeth. "Go back to bed, Ron. This isn't your room."

He makes another whimpering noise but stops pushing. I keep my hand pressed against his chest, regardless. He's wearing navy blue pyjamas, the kind you button up like a shirt, and I can feel the scratchy hair on his chest under my palm.

"I'm so sorry," he whispers.

"Ron! Where are you? What are you doing?" It's Peggy. Thank God for that. I lower my hand as she bustles over to us. She's not wearing her glasses, and this makes her look older for some reason. But I'm pleased she won't get a good look at me as I glance down and realise I'm only wearing knickers and an old t-shirt.

"I was just… I think I was trying to…" Ron stammers. He looks at me as if he's never seen me before then turns to Peggy who is now standing behind him. "What's going on, Peg?"

"You were sleepwalking again," she tells him curtly. "Come on, back to bed with you." She grabs his arm and yanks him around the side of her before addressing me. "I'm very sorry, duck. He does this sometimes. He's harmless though, I promise. What was he saying to you?"

I realise my mouth is hanging open. I close it and open it a few times as if limbering up to reply. It takes me a few goes before I manage to get any words out.

"He was talking about Charlotte," I say. "I think he was a bit confused about who I was. Maybe it's because we look a bit similar?" I say this despite the fact I see no resemblance between me and their daughter in any of the many photos they have of her.

"Oh, Ron. You silly sod," Peggy scolds.

"I was just going to the bathroom," I say. "If you'll excuse me." I sidestep around the two of them and hurry across the landing, making sure I bolt the door before sitting on the toilet just in time. As I pee, I close my eyes, trying to lull myself back into a state of pre-sleep. I can't afford to lie awake for the next few hours. Tomorrow is a big day for me.

I flush and wash my hands but as I open the door onto the landing, I'm dismayed to see Peggy and Ron are still standing outside my room.

"My Charlotte," Ron whines. "Is she coming home?"

"Yes. Soon," Peggy tells him. She sees me and smiles. "I'm sorry," she whispers as she herds her husband past me. "I think he must have been dreaming about her. He misses her when she's not here. We both do. I think that's part of it."

To highlight this, as they pass Charlotte's room Ron reaches out and scratches at her door, the same way he was doing at mine. It could be perfectly innocent but seeing him do it creeps me out. I focus on the patterned carpet to divert my attention from the glut of unsettling thoughts forming in my mind. Is this something he used to do when Charlotte lived here? Did he try to force himself into her room the way he did mine? Is that why she left home? Is that why she put a lock on her bedroom door?

I shudder. But that makes no sense. The padlock is on the outside of the door. Puffing out a long sigh I watch Peggy and Ron stumble across the landing to their room and then close my door.

What the hell am I still doing here?

Even though I'm exhausted I make sure I slide both dead-bolts home and lock the door before climbing into bed and pulling the covers over me. Everything will look different in the morning, I tell myself. I might even be able to laugh about this. But as I scrunch down in the bed, my heart is still pounding.

Why me?

Why do I have to be put up in this weird house?

I should be in Samstone Manor right now, alongside Marsha with the good hair and Katherine with a K, getting a good night's sleep ready for tomorrow's session. Don't I deserve some luxury after everything I've gone through recently?

But I also know that thinking this way - focusing on what you don't have - is pointless at best and can mess your head up if you don't catch it early. I'm lucky to have a job and an employer who is paying for me to get a qualification. I can put up with Ron's sleepwalking for a few more nights. I'm only here for three more after this one.

Three more nights. I can do this.

For now, that can be my new mantra.

FIFTEEN

Something has happened. Something has gone very wrong.

As my mind flickers back online, I blink my eyes open and immediately wish I hadn't. My head feels as if it's full of cotton wool and I have a searing pain in my temples. The room is stark and white, illuminated by the bright sunshine filtering through the curtains.

But this isn't my room.

This isn't my bed.

"Bloody hell!" I force my eyes open and sit upright, "No. Please, no." I reach for my phone and check the time. It's 8:23 a.m. I didn't set my alarm! Why the hell didn't I set my alarm?

Shit.

It all comes rushing back to me. Dinner with Pete. The two large glasses of pinot grigio I drank. That's why I forgot to set my alarm and why my mouth feels as if I've been licking sandpaper. As more memories come back to me, I shudder, remembering my early-morning wake-up call from Ron. I don't know how I feel about what happened but I've no time to consider it too deeply right now, I've got to get up and get to my course. A bus leaves in fifteen minutes which will get me to the venue in time. I can make it, but it's going to be tight.

I leap out of bed and change my underwear before spraying myself liberally with deodorant. It's not ideal but I've no time to even have a sink wash never mind a shower. I pull on a smart pair of black trousers and grab my red shirt with the white piping from the wardrobe. Once dressed I grab my phone and my bag, checking my laptop and notes from yesterday are still in there, before opening my bedroom door.

The landing area is silent and still as I step out and hurry across to the bathroom. Once there I use the toilet and have a ridiculously long pee which I imagine is my bladder mocking me.

You shouldn't have drunk so much water, should you?

It's not like it did me any good. My head is banging.

I finish off and fasten up my trousers before moving over to the sink and opening the door of the cabinet. I find a small bottle of bright purple mouthwash. It looks odd and tastes the way hospitals smell but it'll do the trick. I feel grotty as hell for not even cleaning my teeth, but my toilet bag is in my room and I've no time to spare.

I spit the mouthwash into the sink and gulp water from the tap before checking myself in the mirror. Thankfully I don't look as bad as I imagined I would. My hair is frizzy and I have dark circles under my eyes but I don't look a total wreck. If I keep hydrated, I should get through the day without a problem. I lick my fingers and flatten my hair as best I can and then grab my bag and scurry downstairs.

As I reach the hallway, I hear sounds coming from the kitchen - the chink of crockery and running water, a radio playing a song I can't quite hear. I lean around the side of the banister to see Peggy standing at the sink and Ron sitting in his usual seat at the table. I so want to sneak out without having to deal with either of them, but I know before I even check that the door will be locked and – yes– there's no key in sight.

"Excuse me!" I call out, walking partway towards the kitchen. "Can you let me out, please? I'm in a bit of a rush and need to leave."

Peggy turns off the tap and turns around. "What is it dear?"

"Can you open the door? I'm running late. I need to go." I sound snappy and I sense the people pleaser inside of me tightening with tension, but I don't care. I haven't the energy or the time to bring up what happened last night with Ron. I'm hoping it was a one-off. It had better be. I step back and fold my arms as Peggy shuffles out of the kitchen and heads for the door.

"I am sorry, ducky. Is it locked?"

"Yes! It's always locked. You keep telling me you're going to get me a key. Is there one I can have?"

Peggy looks at me and her mouth flaps as if I've just asked her for a kidney. A liver-spotted hand goes into the pocket of her off-white waffle weave dressing gown and pulls out a key.

"This is my key," she says, shuffling over to the door. "But there is a spare one. In the kitchen, I think. If you wait here, I can have a look for it for you." She unlocks the door and gives me such a sweet smile I can't help but reciprocate.

"No. It's okay. I don't have time to wait," I say, imagining she'll take her sweet time looking in every drawer. "Can you find it for me for this evening? Is that okay?"

She nods and smiles and I mirror her in the hope this might somehow solidify my request in her mind.

"Thank you," I tell her slipping through the gap in the door whilst maintaining eye contact. "Please don't forget. I do need that key."

"Have a good day, dear."

I leave and hurry down the street. Google Maps says it's a five-minute walk to the bus stop but I power walk the whole way and it takes me less than three. By the time I reach the roadside, I'm sweating. Another woman about my age is waiting there too, so I know I haven't missed it. There's no sign of Pete, but why would there be? He catches the earlier bus. I'm surprised at how disappointed I am he's not here but it's probably for the best. I'm sweaty and unwashed and I've not even cleaned my teeth. If I didn't scare him off with my histrionics last night my grotty appearance would certainly do it.

I shake my head, bemused and a little angry at myself I'm even having these thoughts. Pete was friendly and showed a bit of interest in me, that's all. This is not the start of some life-changing romance. Yes, he's handsome and he has a certain charm. But I'm off men. I'm off humans after this week. Which, I realise, isn't great for someone about to launch their new career as a Human Resources Professional, but there you go.

What a joke I am. I can't help but laugh to myself but at least I made it here on time. As the bus appears at the end of the street, I ready myself to board. I know it's more than likely my hangover driving these negative thoughts, but that knowledge doesn't help as the bus pulls up and I'm faced with the prospect of another long day of stress and pressure. But screw it. This is why I'm here. I have to make the most of it.

I'm reminded of an old phrase Nana Mary would often use, whenever something bad happened.

If you don't laugh, you'll cry.

I never really understood what it meant back then, but now I get it. Because you've got to at least try to focus on the good in life, haven't you? Even if only a tiny glimmer of hope sparkles on the horizon, you owe it to yourself to keep your eyes on it. To always be walking towards it. Otherwise, you're just lost in the darkness. And I know what that feels like. I don't ever want to go there again.

SIXTEEN

I get to Samstone Manor with a few minutes to spare and rush down the corridor to the lecture theatre like a woman possessed. As I burst through the door and discover the other attendees mingling around and chatting I can't help but feel a little over dramatic. But that's me I suppose - obsessive imagination, people pleaser, total drama queen.

What did Graham ever see in me?

It doesn't help that everyone seems even more friendly with one another than they were yesterday. I slink over to the refreshment table and watch as other latecomers enter the room and are greeted with waves and smiles. I didn't get any of that. Even timid Katherine with a K has been accepted into a group and appears more vocal and affable this morning. But screw her. Screw everyone. I'm not here to make friends. I'm here to get this qualification and start the next chapter of my life.

The first module today is *Coaching and Mentoring In The Workplace*, which I find a much more interesting topic than those covered yesterday, but no less intense. In the introductory lecture and subsequent discussion, everyone seems so knowledgeable. But my head spins with all the new information I've been presented with. By 11:15 a.m. my hands are aching from all the speed-typing of notes I've done so I'm pleased when the tutor announces the next section will involve a practical element. I feel less pleased, however, when I hear the dreaded words 'role-play'.

They never told me there'd be role-play!

I can't do role-play!

We're divided up into pairs and I'm put with a stout woman called Adie who has short afro hair and kind eyes. The tutor explains each pair will come out to the front in turn and perform a mock coaching session in front of the rest of the group. When I hear this, I turn to Adie and pull a face to show her I'm scared and she responds with just the merest of smiles. Maybe she's shy, but it's not the strong show of solidarity I need right now. I'm so nervous at the thought of acting in front of people I hardly pay attention to the first few role-plays. Instead, I'm up in my head, working out what I'm going to say so I don't make a fool of myself.

When the tutor gestures to Adie and me that it's our turn, we have a hurried discussion and decide I'll be the one to be coached. My hope is if I'm reacting to what she asks me, it'll be easier. As we get up there, however, and I turn to see all the faces staring at us I worry if I'm going to be sick. I need water. I need sleep. I need to be anywhere but here.

After prompting from the tutor, Adie introduces the session and explains what we're going to be doing and asks for my permission to coach me – this is called 'setting up the coaching conversation' and is an important part of the process, we're told. The tutor goes on to explain that there are no right or wrong answers and that I know more about myself than the coach does. Adie is just there to get the best out of me, she says. To help me overcome any hurdles and get me unstuck and moving forward.

Well that all sounds great.

But how long have we got?

I take a deep breath and then we're into the role play. Adie leans forward in her seat and regards me with an involved expression. "What is it you want to talk about today, Lauren?"

Lauren. She's using my real name. I didn't expect that for some reason. I glance at the tutor.

Is this real? Am I supposed to answer truthfully?

She nods eagerly at me as if encouraging me to answer.

"Umm. Well... I have been feeling rather confused lately, about what I'm doing with my life," I say. "I've got a new job and I want to make it work but I'm still stuck in my past. I want to be happy. I want to move on. But I don't know how to."

Whoa!

Where the hell did all that come from?

The second I opened my mouth it poured out of me. I would never normally be that candid with someone I didn't know, especially not in front of a room of strangers, but after a broken night's sleep and still feeling groggy from the wine my defences are down. Yet as Adie nods her head in a supporting manner and asks me what specifically is keeping me stuck, a fresh sense of 'screw it' washes over me. Maybe this coaching session can help me.

Throwing caution to the wind, I tell Adie that I've recently come out of a relationship and moved to a new city for my job. I tell her I'm determined to make it work no matter what and that I wish I could get my ex out of my head. When I've finished, I feel empty but not terrible. It's as if by simply voicing my problems I've released a lot of bad energy. Perhaps there's something in this coaching business after all.

"It sounds to me like you're doing really well," the tutor says, stepping in when Adie becomes lost for words. "Moving to a new city where you don't know anyone is hard enough, but to take on a new job as well... What part of this 'feeling stuck' feeling do you think is your fault?"

I sit back. It feels as if her question has hit me hard in the face. Does she think it's my fault? Is it my fault?

No. It's not!

"None of it's my fault," I say.

"I see. Because if it wasn't your fault, you wouldn't have to do anything to change it, would you?"

"I guess not. I couldn't."

"Do you think that's got something to do with how stuck you feel?"

I stick out my bottom lip. "I don't know."

"What do you want to happen, Lauren?" she asks.

Now there's a question. And one I don't know the answer to. I'm about to tell her this but she second-guesses me.

"What would your answer be to that question if it didn't need to be the right one?"

Huh?

What the hell does that mean?

It feels as if she's doing some sort of mind trickery on me.

"All I'm doing," the tutor says, looking around the room. "Is opening up potential in Lauren's thinking. Sometimes when we get stuck, we close up so tight around the topic we have no perspective. If you can get the coachee to think differently about a topic it can often help them see things from a raised vantage point. So, Lauren - if you didn't have to give a perfect response to that question, how would you answer it? What do you want to happen?"

I swallow. My throat is dry. "I want to be happy."

"Can you be happy in this new situation?" Adie asks, stepping back in.

"I think so. I want to be."

"Good!" She smiles. "And what do you think would be a good first step in achieving that?"

"To stop thinking about my past and stop wishing things were different."

"There we go," the tutor says as if I've just come up with the meaning of life. "To stop wishing things were different. And now you've highlighted this, what's the first good step in achieving it?"

Wow. I sit up and roll my shoulders back as a surge of energy fills me. "When negative thoughts come into my head and I begin to fall back into wishing my life was different I should focus on something else. Something good. Or something I do have control over."

"Excellent. Great catch." The tutor claps her hands together and addresses the room. "Did you see how we only guided Lauren to this conclusion? She came up with it herself. As we've said, the person being coached is the one with all the answers. Your job as a coach is to elicit new thoughts and provide a safe forum for change. Great work, guys, Lauren, Adie. You can sit down now."

I stand, feeling a little woozy suddenly but lighter than I've felt in a long time. The other attendees clap as we go back to our seats and a few of them turn around and give me thumbs up and reassuring smiles. It feels good. I feel good. I can do this. I can.

SEVENTEEN

Unfortunately, the elation I feel post-coaching session doesn't last long. Nor does my resolve to focus on other things when troubling thoughts enter my head. At lunchtime, a few people come up to me and tell me how brave I was and that they hope I feel better soon. They probably mean well but a voice in my head tells me they're being false, and it only makes me feel more distant from everyone. After I've eaten a stodgy jacket potato with cheese in the dining area, I head back to the main space and find everyone is divided up into the same impenetrable cliques as before. I imagine they now have plenty of in-jokes and shared memories to keep them going after spending two nights here. I don't have the motivation to even try infiltrating the gaggling circles.

Do I wish this was different?

I suppose I do.

I blow out a sigh. Trying, and failing, to focus on the good things I have in my life – or on something I do have control over. All at once I feel weighed down by doubt. I doubt myself. I doubt who I was with Graham - and now who I am without him. I doubt this course, my new job, and life in general. Damn it! All the good work I did in this morning's session, all the good energy I experienced crumbles to dust and a familiar sense of dread bubbles up inside of me.

Well, what do you know?

One fifteen-minute mock-coaching session isn't as effective in turning my life around as I thought. It was nice while it lasted but I presume it was nervous energy and adrenaline making me feel good, not a change in circumstances. If it was that easy people wouldn't spend years - and lots of money – in therapy. Not that therapy is the panacea some believe it to be either, in my experience. I've seen three therapists and two counsellors in total and never came out of a session feeling cured or like I'd seen the light. But I was a lot angrier and more nihilistic back then. Maybe I should give therapy another go.

Ha! Maybe I should!

If I ever have the money to pay for it.

And who the hell do I think I am to even contemplate feeling happy?

In this dark state of mind, feeling tired and vulnerable, I have no defences available and my attention soon drifts to the dark recesses of my mind. I've been trying not to think about Ron's visit to my room last night and the creepy way he scratched at Charlotte's door on his way past, but now it's all I can think about.

Was that what he used to do when she lived there?

The way he was scratching at the wood, it was as if he wanted me to know he was there, but without waking Peggy. Ron is far too old and doddery these days to be any kind of threat to me, but he wasn't always feeble and forgetful. I shudder at the idea and tell myself I'm only speculating. It's not good for me to let my imagination run riot in this way. Even so, the thought of staying another three nights in that house troubles me.

Maybe it's time for me to bite the bullet. To stop worrying that I might upset Peggy, or work, and find alternative accommodation for the rest of the week. If I explain to Rochelle that I don't feel comfortable staying at the house - and explain to her what happened last night with Ron - she can't blame me for wanting to stay elsewhere. Can she?

I take out my phone and see from my notifications that I received an email from Rochelle a few minutes earlier. Interesting. Fateful, perhaps? But as I open it up and begin to read my heart sinks and my resolve fades with each line. After a brief greeting, she explains how pleased she is to be working with me and hopes the course is going well. All fine. But then she goes on to apologise for not getting me into the accommodation at Samstone Manor and says how impressed she and her bosses are that I so readily accepted alternative arrangements. It's this resilience, ability to adapt and team spirit that they're always looking for at GP Telecom, she writes.

Well, that's bloody wonderful, isn't it?

There's no way I can reply to that message and tell her I want out of Peggy's place, is there? She'll think I'm a lightweight and mark me as a problem before I even start. And I'm not a lightweight. I might be a people pleaser, but I'm tough when I want to be.

Rochelle finishes the email by saying how she can't wait for me to get my qualification and step into my new role. This should be encouraging for me. I wish it was. I close down my phone and shove it back in my bag.

What's my mantra again?

"Three more nights. I can do this...Bugger."

It's only when I look up and see a woman staring at me, I realise I've been talking out loud. I give her a goofy smile and throw up my eyebrows, but she looks at me like I'm crazy. Maybe I am.

I glance around the room, feeling more alone than I've felt in a long time.

No one cares.

No one is coming to save me.

I'm used to being alone. I've been alone most of my life and I never minded it too much in the past. But that was before I'd experienced the other side of the coin. As thoughts of Graham creep insidiously into my mind, I struggle to hold in my emotions. I look up at the ceiling and open my eyes as wide as they'll go to stop the tears from forming, but it's no use. As I dab at my eyes with the crook of my finger, I see Adie watching me from across the room.

"Are you okay?" she mouths.

I nod and smile but it only makes the tears flow faster. She's being nice to me and I can't take it. Gathering up my things I run from the room and down the corridor to the nearest bathroom. Once there I go to the sink and twist on the tap to splash water on my face. It's ice cold but after the initial shock it's welcome and I go again, washing away my tears and the remnants of yesterday's make-up. When I'm done, I glare at my soggy reflection in the mirror. My eyes are bloodshot, and my nose is red and shiny.

What a mess.

No more wine for you.

And no more thinking about Graham or Pete. Or whatever you think Ron may or may not have done.

"This is your wake-up call," I inform my reflection. "From

now on, you get your head down, you do the work and you get that bloody qualification."

I grab a handful of paper towels from a stack next to the basin and dry my face. The person looking back at me when I'm finished still looks a mess but there's a renewed sparkle in her eyes. How long it will last remains to be seen. You only have to consider the dizzy highs and crashing lows of the last few hours to know I'm more unstable than I realised. But for now, I feel okay.

So far today it's been a rollercoaster ride but there's no point dwelling on the bad parts. Tomorrow is another day and all that jazz. Tonight I'll grab a sandwich on my way back to the house and eat it in my room. I've got my e-reader in my suitcase so I'll get into bed and do some reading. I also remember I have some earplugs in my suitcase. Ron can be outside my room all night tonight if he wants to be, I won't hear him. Then, when I wake up it'll be only two more nights that I have to spend there. Two more nights then a whole lifetime of new possibilities. I toss my hair over my shoulder and smile at myself in the mirror.

I've got this.

I'm strong.

And if you don't laugh, you'll cry, right?

EIGHTEEN

The afternoon session is another dull one, this time on *Recording, Analysing and Using Human Resources Information*.

Yawn!

It's taught by an incredibly tall, skinny woman called Pauline who appears to be driven solely by nervous energy. For most of the session, she stands at the front of the room, reading dryly from her notes on data storage systems whilst flicking through an extensive PowerPoint presentation. The upshot of this is more notetaking. A lot more. I don't think I've ever typed so frantically in my life, but I'm determined to keep up and work to the best of my ability. I'll show Rochelle and GP Telecom how resilient and adaptable I can be. A true team player.

At the end of the session, we're given a test to complete but it's multiple choice and not as hard as I feared it would be. I even finish with twenty minutes to spare, and Pauline has already informed us that once we're done, we can leave for the day. I wait until someone else leaves first, then grab my bag and scurry out of the room. It's a few minutes after five and my next bus isn't until half past, so I grab myself a complimentary bottle of water from the refreshment stand and go sit in the dining area. For want of anything better to do I take out my laptop and search 'Samstone Manor.'

I find the website straight away. It's basic but has some interesting photos of the building throughout the years. I scan-read the text below the main images. It seems the house was built in the fourteenth century but the east wing where I am now and where most of the events take place was rebuilt after it was bombed in the second world war. It goes on to say that the venue has been used for events and luxury weekend breaks since the sixties and also specialises in weddings. When I read this my heart breaks a little, but I try not to dwell on it. I also know it's a bad idea for me to look at the gallery section but curiosity - or perhaps some deep-rooted masochism - gets the better of me. I click on the link and my top lip curls, as I'm presented with a page of brightly coloured thumbnails. I scroll through the photos, moving swiftly past one of the lecture halls but stopping when I get to those showing the bedrooms, bar areas and the many guest lounges. They all look amazing. The rooms are grand and luxurious. Some have four poster beds in them, others have free-standing baths, and they all have mini-bars and televisions. What I wouldn't give for a long hot bath with a gin and tonic later, and then to lose myself in a good film.

I open up another browser window and type in 'Market Allerton hotels'. I know before I hit enter that I'm setting myself up for disappointment, but there's that masochistic streak again. I don't need a therapist to know my recent behaviour points to self-destructive tendencies. I click on the first result, which is a broker site that lists all the available hotels in the area.

"Wow! There we go then," I mutter to myself as I scroll through the available options and view the prices. At first, I think I have them listed out from highest to lowest cost, but no. They're all just incredibly expensive. "Not a chance."

There aren't even any hotels in the actual town of Market Allerton, only big places out of town similar to Samstone Manor. I had hoped there might be a travel lodge or some-where equally as affordable in the area, but no.

I keep scrolling down the list, shaking my head at the astro-nomical prices. It's almost three-hundred pounds to stay one night in some of these places. Even the cheapest option, two hundred and ten pounds per night, is too costly. I have a credit card but it's supposed to be for emergencies only and I've already paid for a round of drinks with it.

Ah, well, it was worth a try.

I close my laptop. It's time for me to catch the bus back to good old Market Allerton and Peggy's television-less spare room. An early night beckons. And, as I reach down for my bag and get a whiff of myself, a shower wouldn't go amiss either.

Now conscious of my two-day-old body odour I'm pleased to discover Pete isn't present for the return leg of my journey either. This bus is earlier than the one I caught yesterday, so that makes sense. I sit on a double seat near the back and place my bag on the seat beside me. I'm aware my actions are selfish and rather anti-social but that's how I feel right now so screw it.

I'm grateful when the bus only fills up with a few passen-gers and I spend the journey looking out the window, counting every blue car we pass in order to keep myself distracted. It's a silly game and childish. But that's how I feel right now, too.

So, screw it.

I get off the bus at the usual spot and go into the nearby off-licence to buy a sandwich. The selection is limited and the chicken salad seems like the safest option. I pay for it, along with a bar of milk chocolate at the counter and stick them in my bag. I'll eat these in my room once I've had a wash and got ready for bed. I just pray the Cliftons are awake and hear me knocking on the door when I get to the house. This is why I need a key. Peggy had better have found me one. My nerves are frayed, and I don't want to have that conversation again.

As I turn the corner and step onto Cranbourne Street, I see an ambulance parked outside number forty-seven. I hasten my step and get up in time to see a female paramedic slamming the back doors shut.

"What happened?" I ask, but my voice comes out hoarse and strangled and I don't think she hears me. She climbs into the front passenger seat and I wander around the back of the vehicle to see Peggy standing in the open doorway of her house wringing her bony hands together. She looks so small and pitiful that I rush straight over to her. "Peggy? Is it Ron?"

She looks up at me and for a moment I feel as if she doesn't know who I am but then she blinks and grabs my arm. "Oh, ducky it was awful. It's his leg. He was in such terrible pain. They think it's broken. They're taking him to the hospital."

"Oh no, that's awful," I say. "Do you want to go with him? I can watch the house." I feel a bit crappy about the sense of relief I feel when I suggest this, but it makes sense for everyone.

Peggy shakes her head. "No. I can't." To help solidify this decision the ambulance siren beeps, and the lights begin to flash. I watch as it pulls away from the curb and drives away. Peggy and I stare after it until it gets to the end of the road and then I turn to look at her.

"Why can't you go with him?"

She moves back into the house. "I need to be here in case Charlotte comes home."

"What?" I follow her inside. "Is she coming here? Tonight?"

"I think so."

"So, you've told her about her dad's injury?" I ask.

Peggy frowns. "No. But it's fine. She'll be here."

"I see. Do you know when?"

Peggy wanders down the hallway without answering. I shut the door behind me and follow her into the kitchen. When I get there, I see the back door hanging open. For some reason, on seeing this, I get a strange fluttering sensation in the pit of my stomach and my curiosity has me step outside to look in the backyard. It's empty but as I turn to renter the house, I see a large dusty footprint on the stoop of the doorway. As I go back inside and shut the door, Peggy is sitting at the table staring out the window.

"Was someone here?" I ask her.

She wrinkles her nose but doesn't look at me. "What? Here?"

"Was someone else in the house, apart from you and Ron?"

"Oh? No... I don't think so."

I pull a chair around and sit adjacent to her. "Are you sure, Peggy? They didn't hurt Ron, did they?"

She doesn't look at me. "Charlotte will be home soon," she says. "She'll sort everything out. She'll make it okay. Ron fell. That's what happened."

I don't know what to believe. Something doesn't feel right.

Peggy's vagueness isn't helping matters but I don't want to push the issue of Ron's injury too hard. She's probably in shock.

"Can I get you anything?" I ask. "A cup of tea? Or some water?"

"No, thank you, dear."

"Did the ambulance people say they'd call to let you know about Ron?" I ask.

Her face crumples as if she's thinking. "I can't remember. I hope so. If Charlotte doesn't come tonight, I'll get a taxi to the hospital in the morning."

"Yes. That sounds like a good idea."

"And don't worry," she says, holding up a wizened finger. "I'll leave you a key for the front door if I set off before you wake up."

I want a bloody key regardless! But I don't say this. It's not the time. And the fact she's remembered about me needing a key bodes well I feel. Even if she is rather ambiguous about what happened to her husband.

I watch her, trying to work out what's going on. "Do you really think Charlotte is coming here tonight?" I ask.

"Maybe," she says and coughs. It's a shrill but hacking cough that sounds as though it's coming out of a much bigger person. I jump up and get her glass of water and carry it over to her. She accepts the glass and takes a sip, but it looks as if the outburst has almost finished her off. "I think I need to lie down," she whispers.

"Yes of course." I help her up. "What about Charlotte?" I ask as we shuffle into the hallway.

"She's got a key."

Oh, Has she?

How wonderful for Charlotte. At least someone has.

But as I help Peggy up the stairs, I can't shake the sense that something is wrong. Either it's got something to do with Ron's injury, or Charlotte's imminent visit, or both. But something is bothering Peggy and now it's bothering me. The problem is I still can't quite put my finger on what it is that so unnerves me. It's as if my subconscious knows something is wrong but it's keeping it from me.

But as I get Peggy up to the landing all these confusing questions and worrying notions fall away.

"Oh?"

I can't believe what I'm seeing. I let out an involuntary gasp and glance down at Peggy, but she doesn't say anything. She's probably too worn out and confused to realise what I'm looking at. But it's there for us both to see. The padlock on the door to Charlotte's room is gone and the door is open.

NINETEEN

I guide Peggy into bed, which isn't the easiest task in the world despite her diminutive size. With my arm around her, I can feel how bony she is. It's as if she hasn't eaten a decent meal in years, yet she drags her feet and is difficult to manoeuver. Eventually, I pull the covers back on the double bed she normally shares with Ron and lower her onto the sagging mattress.

"Stay with me," she says as I lift her legs onto the bed and place the covers over her.

"Umm, I—" I don't want to leave her alone if she's feeling sad and lonely, but I can't stop thinking about the fact Charlotte's door is now unlocked. Did Peggy leave it that way? Did Ron? Is the reason he's now in the hospital linked somehow? My mind is on overdrive and I have to tell myself to calm down. It's probably nothing out of the ordinary. There's probably nothing of interest in the room.

"Please, dear," Peggy says, grabbing my hand in her bony grip. She looks up at me with eyes that are watery and full of pain and how can I say no?

"Sure. I'll stay until you fall asleep," I whisper, lifting her hand off mine and placing it gently on the bed. "Don't worry. Everything is going to be fine."

She smiles and closes her eyes before releasing a long rasping sigh that seems to reduce her size by at least a half. I worry for a moment she's died but then her chest begins to rise and fall gently. I perch on the end of the bed and make myself as comfortable as I can.

As I watch Peggy lying there, looking so peaceful, I'm reminded once more of Nana Mary. We all called her nana, but she wasn't really anyone's nana. Or, if she was, she never mentioned any grandchildren to us. Mary was the head of Gladstone House. She was one of the good ones. Maybe one of the only good ones. I loved her. We all did. She gave good advice and I remember vowing when I left that I'd go back and look for her when I was old enough. To thank her. But life moves on and so does everyone else and I never did go back.

A shiver runs down my body. With my emotions laid raw, my head is suddenly filled with thoughts of Graham. I shake my head. I've got to stop this. I've got to forget about him and move on.

The problem is a part of me doesn't want to. Why would I want to forget about someone I love? Yet I'm aware that this mindset is exactly what is keeping me stuck and unsure of myself. If I could only let go of the idea that we could ever rekindle our love, I'd be able to move on with the rest of my life. It would hurt like hell, I know that. But hurt doesn't last forever. It weakens over time.

Because life moves on and so does everyone else.

I expect this is the case for many people after a heartbreak. They know what path they need to take to get over the other person, yet they wilfully choose another path, the wrong path.

Because this is a path that's familiar to them. Maybe they call it having hope. But I know from experience hope is a dangerous thing to rest your happiness on. It keeps you clinging to an idea that one day things will be different – *better* – but you can cling onto that idea your whole life, and it never does get better. And in the process, life passes you by.

People spend their entire lives hoping their luck will change. They kid themselves that if they really, *really* want something enough it can happen for them.

Because why not? They deserve happiness. Everyone does. Don't they?

But ask any kid from the care system. They'll tell you differently. For many years I'd pray and hope and dream that a nice family would take me on and adopt me. But it never happened and by the time I reached my teens, I started to see how destructive this mindset was. So I stopped believing it would ever happen to me. I stopped hoping.

Why can't I find this same resolve when it comes to Graham?

I stare at Peggy, wondering what she's hoping for right now. For Ron to get better and return home - or maybe not? For Charlotte to return home – or maybe not? Because something is still bothering me about this whole set-up and my curiosity is only growing with the knowledge the mysterious room next door is now accessible.

Peggy seems like such a nice old lady. Obviously, she's got her issues – I detected alcohol on her breath as I was helping her to bed - and perhaps shouldn't let her spare room out to strangers if she's not up to the task. But she's got a good heart. I can tell. At least one of us has. Because I'm desperate for her to fall asleep so I can have a peek into Charlotte's room.

As Peggy's breathing slows and gets heavier I have so

many questions swirling around in my head. Why is the room unlocked, tonight of all nights? Does it have something to do with Ron's injury? I want to know how he broke his leg. Did he fall? Was he pushed? And who is the owner of the dusty footprint in the backyard?

I'm getting ahead of myself, letting my imagination take me to dark places, but I can't help it. When I'm sure Peggy is asleep, I place my feet on the carpet and ease myself slowly off the bed so I don't wake her. Once on my feet, I watch her for a few seconds longer, but she doesn't stir. She's dead to the world, as they say.

Moving stealth-like, and with an eye on Peggy all the time, I make my way out of her bedroom. It's only when I've closed the door and am standing on the landing do I allow myself to breathe.

I move over to Charlotte's room. The door is already open a few inches. I push it all the way open and step inside.

Whoa!

I don't know what I was expecting to find in this room but it's not this.

A single bed stands in the corner opposite the door, which isn't too surprising, but the walls are covered in brightly coloured posters. They're mainly of The Backstreet Boys and NSYNC but there's also a large, framed print of Garfield the cat on the wall above the bed. The curtains are pink with a yellow zig-zag pattern on them and the paper light shade is blue and covered in rainbows. It's weird. Peggy said her daughter was thirty-four, but this is the bedroom of a teenage girl.

I walk into the middle of the room and spin around, trying to work out what it is that bothers me so much about it. It's the teenage décor, sure, but it's something else. As I'm staring at the wardrobe I realise the beige hold-alls I saw through the gap in the door, have gone.

Did I imagine them?

No. They were there. Definitely. Four of them, bulging with what I assumed were old clothes. But maybe I was wrong. I go over to the wardrobe and open both doors. It's empty except for two dresses, which look as if they were bought for a special occasion. A wedding maybe, or a prom, I check the labels. One is a UK size 8. The other says 'Age 14 – 16'.

What the hell is going on here?

I close the wardrobe doors and step back. All at once I feel incredibly uncomfortable and like I shouldn't be here. The last thing I want is for Peggy to find me in her daughter's room. If Charlotte does come back to visit, maybe she has a weird kink where she likes her old room to stay as it always was. Maybe that's why they keep it locked. Each to their own and all that. The dad of my second foster family – the Bernhards – would go into my room when I wasn't there and turn it upside down. He thought I was doing drugs. Or so he said. I wasn't, but I remember feeling violated knowing he'd gone through my underwear and my private things. Not that I had much of anything to call my own. But it was the principle, and I don't want to be intrusive here. It's not for me to judge what Peggy's daughter is into. Yet there is something about this room, and this house, that bothers me a great deal.

What is the story here…?

Then it hits me. This looks like the room of a teenage girl because it is the room of a teenage girl. At first, Ron told me Charlotte was twenty-eight but later Peggy said she was actually thirty-four. No big deal there. It's clear Ron has severe memory issues. But whether Charlotte is twenty-eight or thirty-four it makes no difference. Because, despite there being so many photos of her hanging on the walls in this house, she's never older than sixteen in any of them.

The implications of this land heavy on my shoulders and I stagger over to the bed and sit on the edge. I feel woozy suddenly and swallow back mouthfuls of air to stop myself from being sick.

This is the room of a sixteen-year-old girl…

Charlotte is never older than sixteen in any of the photos…

Which to me can mean only one of two things. Either Charlotte ran away from home eighteen years ago. Or she's dead.

TWENTY

P oor Charlotte. And poor Peggy, too. All this time, has she kept Charlotte's room so preserved out of grief? As a memorial to her daughter's memory? But then I remember her mentioning how Charlotte had moved to Liverpool to pursue nursing school. Was this made up or does Peggy actually believe that happened? A chill crawls over my skin as I consider Ron and his creepy night calls. Is that why Charlotte ran away?

I shake my head free of these unanswerable questions and get up off the bed. I feel so confused I'm dizzy but I don't have the first idea what to do with any of this new information. But then, do I need to do anything at all? I'm only here for a few more days and even if Charlotte is dead, it doesn't mean that anything untoward happened here. People cope with the death of a loved one in many different ways. Keeping Charlotte's bedroom decorated the way it was when she was alive could be how Peggy and Ron feel closest to her. I'm sure it happens a lot with grieving parents.

I look around the room, searching for proof of my theory

that Charlotte is indeed dead. I can't help but feel this is the most likely scenario. But would they keep proof of her death in here? And what would it look like?

I walk over to the old desk and slide the top drawer open. Except for a few dust bunnies and a faded gas safety certificate, it's empty. The story is the same in the remaining three drawers. I find some batteries, a naked Barbie with marker pen scribbled on her face and an old notepad full of doodles, but nothing to indicate Charlotte's fate.

I slide the last drawer closed and glance around the room before flattening the bed sheets where I was sitting just now. I already feel bad being in here and want to leave the place exactly as I found it.

I stand to leave when I hear a yell from next door.

"Ron! Charlotte!"

It makes me jump. It's Peggy, but her voice is so high-pitched and forceful that she sounds different. Composing myself I hurry out of the room and ease the door shut. Once on the landing, I hear her again, screaming out the names of her loved ones like a banshee wail.

"Hey, hey, it's okay. I'm here," I say, going into her room.

Peggy is lying in bed with the covers over her but is thrashing around like she's having some sort of fit. It's rather unsettling and I don't know what to do.

"Charlotte! My Charlotte!" I go to her and grab her hand.

"It's me. It's Lau… It's Charlotte." I have no idea what compels me to say this but as I do, she stops thrashing and snaps her head to look at me.

"It's you." I'm not sure if it's a question or not. It doesn't sound like one. "You came back. You said you would. Where's your dad?"

The way she looks at me it's as if she's looking through me

and I wonder if she's delirious or dreaming. One of the girls I was in care with would have weird episodes at night where she sat up in bed and talked to you as if she was awake. But in the morning she had no recollection of any of it. We used to find it funny and get her to say dumb things so we could tease her the next day. But this isn't funny.

"Ron is in hospital, remember?" I whisper. "He hurt his leg. He's fine."

"Did he fall?"

I gnaw at my top lip as I consider how to reply. Is it possible she might fill me in on the situation if I press her on it? Or is that me being manipulative?

"I'm not sure," I say. "I wasn't there. But you were. Do you remember what happened to him, Peggy?"

She screws her face up. "No. I don't." She looks panicked and I stroke the back of her hand to calm her.

"That's okay. He's fine. You can go see him in the morning. And I'm here. You're safe."

Peggy smiles. "How are you?"

I clear my throat. "I'm....good. I've been in Liverpool."

"Liverpool?"

"Yes. That's where I live."

"Is it?"

"Yes, Mum." As I say this I tense and get a nasty feeling as if I've overstepped. But I'm here now and I can't stop myself. "Do you know otherwise?"

Peggy closes her eyes and her lips tremble. "I don't know."

"What happened to me?" I whisper and then when she doesn't respond. "What happened to Charlotte, Peggy?"

Her nose twitches but she doesn't speak or open her eyes. A moment later she lets out a low purring noise and I wonder if she's fallen asleep. It's frustrating being this close to the truth and getting nowhere, but maybe it's for the best. I step back and turn towards the door when Peggy makes a soft whimpering sound.

"I'm so sorry, darling," she mutters. "I'm so sorry..."

I spin back around. Her eyes are closed and she looks peaceful.

"What are you sorry for?" I ask. "Peggy? Mum? What are you sorry for?"

I need to know the answer to this question. If she thinks I'm Charlotte, then why is she apologising so profusely?

What did she do?

What did they do?

A bustle of unhelpful notions and ideas fogs my mind as I stare down at Peggy. She looks so innocent lying there. But is she? Or did she and Ron kill Charlotte? I realise I know nothing about this old couple. I still don't believe they're a threat to me. But maybe once they were a threat to someone. Maybe nineteen years ago, when they were both younger and stronger.

I think about all the times Peggy and Ron told me I looked like Charlotte. Do they want me to be her? Have there been others before me?

Bloody hell!

The thought sends me spiralling and I leave Peggy's room and hurry across the landing to my room. Once there I close the door and lock it before sliding the bolts across and sitting on the end of the bed.

Nineteen years. What if there really have been other girls? Charlotte substitutes. This could be one of those houses of horror you hear about, with a dozen bodies buried under the backyard. It's not beyond the realms of possibility. Ron and Peggy are old and forgetful but that doesn't mean they weren't once monsters. This could be them playing out their old ways, inviting young women to stay in their spare room as a replacement for their dead daughter. Right up until the point that they...

No! Stop it, Lauren!

This is ludicrous!

I realise my breathing has become short and rapid as if I'm about to hyperventilate. I consciously suck back a deep breath and hold it in my chest for a count of five before releasing it. This calms me enough I'm able to shake myself free from my feverish imagination.

I'm being pathetic, I tell myself. This is all in my head. I'm tired and emotional and I need some sleep. As I undress down to my underwear and pull my sleepshirt over my head I also wonder if a small part of me relishes the drama. Because, if I'm worried about what happened to Charlotte then I don't have to think about Graham. By the time I've had a drink of water and set my alarm for the morning, I've almost convinced myself this is the case. I'm safe here in this room. No one can get to me here. But that doesn't stop me from checking the door is locked and bolted for the second time in as many minutes before I climb into bed.

TWENTY-ONE

I wake up in a cold sweat. As my eyelids flicker open, I'm presented with a room that is pitch dark. No light comes in even under the gap in the curtains. It's still dark outside. Not time to wake up yet. I close my eyes, glad of this fact despite feeling anxious. Was I dreaming just now? I can't remember.

But something feels wrong.

A faded memory at the edge of my awareness torments me. I get the impression it wants me to fully wake up and focus on it but the bed is so warm and the covers soft and heavy. I'm safe here. And I'm tired. I need more sleep. In this drowsy state, not quite awake but not fully asleep my brain struggles to make sense of things.

Go back to sleep, I tell myself.

My alarm is set. I've nothing to worry about. I let out a sigh to try to reset my mood and fall back asleep. But as my awareness spreads beyond the bed, I hear voices. In my dreamy haze, I can't place where they're coming from, only that they're men's voices. Is it Pete? Does it sound like Pete? Is he here? Is he in the house, somewhere?

I wish he was here in this bed.

I smile to myself as reason wanes and oblivion washes over me.

Sleep.

Sleep is nice.

Sleep is good…

Sleep is…

My eyes snap open on the first chime of my alarm. I reach for my phone and switch it off, already wide awake and alert. I glance around the room and stretch. That's when it all comes rushing back to me.

The room.

Charlotte.

Poor Charlotte.

Although, I don't even know for sure if she is dead. In the friendly light of day, the paranoid, macabre nonsense that was going through my head last night seems even more preposterous. I climb out of bed and stretch my arms wide. Whatever has happened in this house, wherever Charlotte Clifton is, it's none of my business and I make a promise to myself to not concern myself with her any longer. I've only two more nights here and then I'm gone and if I did feel a bit creeped out by Ron, he's in hospital so what's the worst that can happen?

I grab my towel and open my bedroom door. The landing area is quiet and the door to Peggy's room is closed. I walk over to it and put my ear to the wood. I can't hear anything, so I tap my knuckle on the wood and whisper her name.

"Peggy? Are you awake?"

There's no answer. I give it another few seconds, ease open the door and put my head around the side. The curtains are open and the bed is perfectly made but Peggy is nowhere to be seen. Considering how muddled and wearied she seemed last night this strikes me as odd. I reason she must have got up early and is now downstairs pottering around. With this in mind, I head into the bathroom for a shower.

As I'm washing it dawns on me that Peggy mentioned she might go to the hospital this morning to see Ron. But it wouldn't be this early, would it? I finish off in the shower and brush my teeth before wrapping my towel around me and heading back to my room. On the way, I lean over the side of the stairwell to listen for movement down below. I can't hear anything but if Peggy is sitting in the kitchen having her breakfast there's no reason why I would.

I dry myself and get dressed. Once I've put on a bit of make-up and have packed my bag, I head downstairs, reassuring myself as I go that all will be well. I do this right until I get into the kitchen and find it devoid of both Peggy and the front door key that she promised she'd leave for me.

"Shit," I sneer, through gritted teeth. "I don't need this today!"

I place my bag on the kitchen table and march back down the hallway to check the front door. It's locked. Why would I expect anything else? Cursing Peggy under my breath I do a quick tour of the downstairs rooms, scanning every surface for a note or a key. I find nothing and return to the kitchen empty-handed.

"Peggy!" I call out. But unless she's hiding in another secret room of theirs that I'm unaware of, she's not here. "What the bloody hell do I do now, Peggy?" I yell into the ceiling.

I check my phone. The clock on the screen shows it's 8:19 a.m. I've got twenty minutes to get to the bus stop.

I look around, searching for a way out, an escape route. I

try the back door but it too is locked and there is no key in sight. For heaven's sake. I need to get out of here. I need to get to my course. If I screw it up I can kiss my job goodbye and any chance of a fresh start in Manchester. I've no idea what I'll do if that happens. I've got no money, no family. I've not even got friends I can lean on.

No! It can't happen!

I have to get to the bus stop. Right now.

The back door has a pane of glass in the top panel that's big enough for me to fit through. I consider picking up a mug off the draining board and chucking it at the glass. Smashing it would make me feel a lot better, but it could also get me in trouble with work if they've put down a deposit on the booking. Plus, I've already been branded the course weirdo. I don't fancy turning up cut to ribbons from any shards of glass that remain sticking out of the doorframe. I survey the kitchen and my eyes land on the window above the sink.

The top panel is long and slim but looks as if it opens out all the way on an old hinge. It's going to be a tight squeeze, but I reckon I could fit through at a push. That's my exit. It's all I've got.

Praying that sheer determination will save the day I grab my bag and clamber up onto the worktop, grabbing the silver neck of the mixer tap to steady myself. Once there I unhook the window clasp and push at the frame. It's stiff as if it hasn't been used in many years, but I manage to get it open. A waft of cool morning air hits me in the face, followed by the sounds and smells of the outside world. Somewhere a car horn beeps and the warm toasty smell of boiler steam drifts into the back-yard from a neighbouring house. Assessing the width of the window a final time I fling my bag out of the window and grab onto the wooden frame to haul myself up. My legs swing through the air, searching for purchase and my right one finds the mixer tap which I use to push myself up and get my head and shoulders through the gap. Thankfully I've always been rather slim in build and if I've got my head through, I reason the rest of me will follow. Or is that just cats? Either way, I get enough of my upper body through the window that the momentum helps the rest of me to slide out. But now I'm headfirst facing the concrete slabs of the back yard and I worry I'm going to hurt myself. I reach out with my hands and grab hold of the windowsill, so I'm now doing a sort of handstand with my feet still in the house and only the bottom of my calves pressing against the window frame to stop me from falling out.

For heaven's sake, Lauren.

How the hell have you got yourself into this mess?

I remain in this position while I work out my best plan of action. I've got about ten minutes before my bus arrives, but I don't want to rush and end up joining Ron in the hospital.

I've got to somehow vault over onto my feet. I'm no gymnast but it's the only way I can see this working. Otherwise, I'm going to be stuck here and the blood is already rushing to my head. Before I can talk myself out of it I unhook my feet from inside the window frame and allow my feet to sway over my head, taking me off balance. The inertia carries me over and as I feel my lower body falling, I push off from the windowsill and flip myself forward. The world spins away from me, the colours and shapes morphing into a blur of white before I land with a thud on my arse with one of my legs bent under me. As the backyard swims into focus I burst out laughing.

I did it. I'm free.

I check myself. I've no broken bones as far as I can tell and I can't even feel any pain, not even in my leg. I get up and brush myself down, looking over my shoulder at the window. It's shut itself after me but isn't on the latch. A plucky burglar of diminutive size could get into the house if they wanted to. But what would they get away with if they did? An old television? As many photos as they could carry of the sixteen-year-old Charlotte? Besides, it's not my fault Peggy didn't leave me a key. I did ask her for one.

Oh, did I ask!

Still feeling jumpy and excitable from the fight-or-flight hormones racing through my system, I pick up my bag and head for the gate on the far side of the yard. As I get there, I have a sinking feeling that this too may be locked but it's only via a deadbolt that I slide open easily enough. This is not the sort of security measures I've come to expect from the Cliftons, but I hardly take note as I open the gate and head out into the narrow alleyway beyond. As I go, I pull out my phone to check the time. It's 8:28 a.m. I've got twelve minutes to get to the bus stop. I can do this. I set off walking when I hear a noise over my shoulder that makes me jump. It's just a cat, I tell myself. Or a neighbour putting out their bins. But before I can turn around, I feel a weight on my shoulder and let out a yelp as a hand grabs me.

TWENTY-TWO

I spin around. The muscles in my shoulders and across my chest tighten as my hands instinctively curl into claws. "Get the hell off of me I—"

"Whoa! Careful, Lauren. It's only me!" My assailant lets go of me and jumps away holding his hands up.

As my vicious, survival instincts dwindle, I realise it's Pete. "Bloody hell. You scared the life out of me!"

"Yeah. My bad. I shouldn't have grabbed you. I'm so sorry. But I did call your name a few times, but you didn't stop."

I gasp. I never heard him. I was probably too up in my head for it to register. I glance around, feeling my chest rising and falling as I try to catch my breath. "What are you doing here?"

"I was in my backyard putting some rubbish out and I saw you climbing out the window. I didn't know if you needed help. So…" He looks down and away as if he's embarrassed.

Or is it something else?

I recollect hearing his voice this morning, but as I stand here now, I don't know if it was real or part of a dream. An unsettling notion hits me that he's been watching me, that his being here now is no coincidence. Could Pete have something to do with the strange goings-on at Peggy's house? Could that footprint I saw be his? Was he the one who hurt Ron? Then I recount the warmth and excitement I felt when I imagined him in bed with me and I have to turn away lest the memory shows on my face.

Jesus.

My messed-up, dual personality strikes again. I wanted him so much at that moment. And now I'm wondering if he's a threat.

Maybe I am a masochist.

Maybe this is what turns me on these days?

Cursing myself and defiant that I will not be another care home kid cliché I turn around and set off walking down the alleyway.

"Sorry. I've got to catch my bus," I call back over my shoulder "I'm late. I'll see you around."

"Lauren! Wait. I'll come with you." As I take a right towards the street, he hurries after me. "Is everything all right? You seem tense?"

"Well, I did just have to climb out of the window," I reply, not turning around.

"What happened? Where are the old couple?"

I sigh. I don't want to be doing this but he's persistent. "Ron, the husband, is in the hospital. I think Peggy must have left early to go and visit him."

"Wow. That is early," Pete says. "Do they have visiting hours at this time of day?"

I slow down. That's a good point. And I have no idea how the visiting system works. Maybe because she's old and next of kin they allow it. I look up at Pete. Considering his question has quietened my racing mind enough I don't feel like I need to get away from him quite so readily.

"Were you spying on me?" I ask him.

"What do you mean?"

"I don't know. Sorry. There are just a lot of bizarre things going on around here. I can't work out if I'm right to feel paranoid or I'm just overthinking everything." I shrug. "You don't need to hear all this. Forget it."

"No, it's fine," he says, keeping up with me as I quicken my pace. "Why don't you tell me what's going on and I'll see if I can help."

"How can you help?"

"I don't know. But I find talking about a problem out loud can help."

I go up in my head and make a quick judgement of the situation. I don't think I should trust Pete but only because I don't think I should trust anyone right now. Still, as I gaze into his eyes I don't detect any malice or hostility. I notice his eyes are a rich blue colour, like the Mediterranean sea. In fact, they're rather unusual. The sort of eyes you could get lost in…*Stop it!*

This is not the time!

We come out on Cranbourne Street and I cross over.

"I don't know what to say," I tell him. "They have this room in their house that was locked when I arrived. They said it belonged to their daughter, Charlotte, and that she stayed over when she visited. But last night the door to the room was open and I went in. It's as if the whole room has been preserved for twenty years. There are still boy band posters on the wall, from when Charlotte was a teenager. But she's supposedly thirty-four now."

We take a left at the end of the street and head down the

next one towards the main road. We're walking fast and with no food inside of me, I feel faint and nauseous.

"What do you think is going on?" Pete asks as we take the next left and I see the bus stop in front of us.

"I think Charlotte might be dead," I say. "And either Peggy and Ron can't accept it and are keeping a shrine to her or... shit, I don't know. I probably sound like a nut job to you."

"No. You don't. Honestly."

He doesn't sound convincing. I grimace. "Yeah. I do. I think I'm just tired and paranoid. Please forget I ever said anything."

"No, no. I believe you," he says. "The door was locked but you got inside. What else did you see in there apart from the posters? Was there anything out of the ordinary?"

He's staring at me with such a troubled expression on his face it spurs me on to tell him.

"There was some old furniture and a single bed. That's it. When I looked through the crack in the door a day earlier there were some bags piled next to the wardrobe, but they weren't there last night. I assumed they were full of old clothing. Maybe Peggy decided it was too much to bear and threw them out."

Yet, even as I say this it sounds wrong. Why conserve your daughter's room exactly as it was for nearly two decades only to suddenly clear it out?

Shit.

Unless I am right. Unless she and Ron are hoping I'll become a replacement.

I screw my face up to stop the thought from fully forming. If I told Pete what I was thinking about he'd laugh in my face, I'm sure of it.

Once I reach the bus stop, I cast my attention down the main strip and see the bus appear from around the corner at the far end. Thank God. I made it here in time. I look at Pete who appears to be deep in thought.

"How many bags?" he asks.

"What? Oh, four. But like I say, they've gone."

He nods but a deep frown creases his forehead. "And no one else has been in the house as far as you're aware?"

I stop walking. I don't know whether it's the question or the serious tone of Pete's voice that unsettles me. As I glance from the bus back to him he's staring at me and there's an intensity in his eyes that unnerves me.

What is he thinking about?

Is he concerned about my well-being, or something else?

As I'm assessing what to do the bus pulls up and I hurry down and join the queue of people to get on. We can talk some more on the journey to work. I'll feel more secure sharing my concerns with him when surrounded by other passengers. But as it gets to my turn and I step up onto the bus, I turn back to see Pete standing a few feet from the roadside.

"Aren't you getting on?" I call out to him.

He shakes his head. "I'm working from home this morning."

"Oh. Why did you…? You didn't have to…?" I splutter. "I thought you were catching the same bus."

He smiles, and I can't help but feel it's one full of warmth. "It's fine," he says, raising his chin. "I fancied some fresh air. And I wanted to talk to you. I wanted to see you again."

I smile back and want him to say more, but the driver catches my eye and gives me a harsh stare. "Well, it was nice to see you," I tell Pete.

"Yes. You too. Maybe I'll see you later?"

I step up onto the bus feeling more confused than ever. "Yeah," I call back. "Maybe."

TWENTY-THREE

The first module today is on *Supporting Good Practice and Reward Management.* I reckon I deserve a big reward after enduring all I have done this week so far. It'll be worth it, to get this damn qualification, but I'm not there yet. I still have to brave two more nights in Peggy's spare room.

What a lucky girl I am.

If the room wasn't so secure with the lock and deadbolts on the door, I might feel warier than I do. But I'm tough and I've endured worse places in my lifetime. There have been scarier houses, scarier bedrooms and much scarier people. And that was when I was a kid. Now I'm a grown woman. I can survive two more nights of awkwardness and unease. Then I'll have the certification under my belt and be a fully-fledged HR Professional.

There'll be no stopping me.

With that in mind I knuckle down for the rest of the day, focusing my attention on the lectures and practical work I'm tasked with, rather than the strange goings on at forty-seven

Cranbourne Street. It feels good to be working hard, knowing I'm bettering myself in the process and by the time the last session of the day is complete, I'm exhausted but proud of myself.

As I wait for the bus to take me back to Market Allerton I allow my thoughts to drift onto Pete. I might be doubting my instincts currently, but I'm certain I'd pick up on it if he had an ulterior motive. I'd even go as far as to say he's a good guy and if he does come across as a bit intense at times it's only because he's lonely and unsure of himself after the break-up of his relationship.

This doesn't explain why I thought I heard his voice in the early hours of this morning. However, as the day goes on, I'm more convinced than ever it was just part of my dream. Which actually turned into quite a nice dream in the end, I seem to remember.

I'm still in this mindset when the bus pulls up and, when I climb on and don't see Pete waiting for me, my heart sinks. He said he was working at home this morning. He didn't say anything about the afternoon. I thought he'd be here.

I wanted him to be here.

I shuffle onto the edge of the nearest seat, which is already occupied by an old man with wet lips and droopy eyes. He mutters something under his breath as I make myself comfortable, but I don't catch it.

The rest of the bus ride is uneventful, and I spend the journey with my eyes closed, resetting my system. We were set an assignment linked to this morning's module – to create a pamphlet on reward systems - but I completed it during my lunch hour. I like to get things out of the way rather than have them hanging over me and it wasn't like I had anything better to do on my lunch hour. No one talks to the course outcast. I also think a part of me was counting on an after-work drink with Pete being on the cards. Obviously, I was wrong, and while I'm pleased the assignment is out of the way, it does leave me with an entire evening with nothing to do.

I get off the bus at my stop and I venture once more into the off-licence to buy myself another sandwich. I opt for egg mayonnaise this time – no chocolate – and then take my time strolling back to the house. As I reach Cranbourne Street, I wonder about knocking on Pete's door to see if he wants to go to the pub – but as I get to his house, I walk straight past it. Is this my instincts taking over or just my awkwardness?

Either way, it's probably for the best.

The curtains in Peggy's front room are open as I get up to the house and I see a flash of movement behind the glass. I take this as a good sign and knock on the front door to be let in. As I wait, I hear more movement coming from the hallway on the other side. A shuffling noise and whispered voices. I step up to the door to try to see through the frosted glass and as I'm doing so the door opens to reveal Peggy's crumpled face.

"Oh, it's you, ducky. Come in." She shuffles backwards and beckons me inside, displaying an eagerness I've not experienced from her before. I step into the house and shut the door behind me.

"How are you?" I ask.

"Not so bad, thank you."

"I take it you were at the hospital this morning?" I ask. When she looks puzzled, I add. "It's just I was locked in and didn't have a key. I almost missed my bus."

"Oh my gosh! I am sorry, dear. Whatever did you do?"

"I climbed out the kitchen window," I say. My voice sounds curt, but the way Peggy looks up at me – twisting her lips to one side the same way Nana Mary would when she was thinking hard about something - I can't stay angry with her. "It's fine. I made it to the stop. How is Ron?"

"Ron?"

I grit my teeth. "Did you go visit him?"

She frowns. "Oh. Yes. The hospital. He's broken his ankle poor soul. They said they need to do some more tests on him. Or something like that. They said they need to keep him in for another day."

"Well, he's in the best place."

"Yes." Peggy hobbles through into the front room. I think about going straight upstairs to my room, but I'm compelled to follow her.

"Was it nice to see him?" I ask as she lowers herself into her armchair. It looks as if it pains her to move and I go over to help her.

"Who?" she says, as I put my arm around her and lower her into the chair.

"Ron."

"Oh... Yes..." She sighs and I detect a strong whiff of alcohol on her breath.

Ah, Peggy. Again?

Is this what causes her night-time haziness?

I get her settled in the chair and step over to the doorway. "Do you want a glass of water?" I ask.

She frowns and makes a scoffing noise as if this is the weirdest question anyone has ever asked her. I notice her hands are shaking.

"Peggy?" She looks up and through me. "A glass of water?"

She nods. "Thank you."

I leave her and go to the kitchen. There are two glasses

already on the table and an empty plastic shopping bag. A bottle of vodka stands next to the sink which I assume was brought here in the shopping bag. But two glasses? I have to assume Peggy got them out and then forgot what she was doing. I pick them up in turn. They look clean and neither glass has an odour. I never bought the idea vodka doesn't smell. I've known at least two people who drank it, and I could always smell it on them. I pick up the bottle off the side and examine it. I don't know what depresses me more, the fact it's already half empty or that it's a cheap brand.

I place it in one of the cupboards and rinse the glasses before filling them both with water. I'm about to carry them through into the front room when I see the back door is open a crack. I place the glasses down and go over to it. There are more dusty footsteps on the lino in front of the door. Big footprints. Men's footprints.

I close the door and grab the glasses of water. "Peggy, has someone else been here?" I ask as I go through into the front room.

Peggy sits up as if startled. Her mouth flaps as if she's trying to form words but can't. "Some—Someone else?" she stammers.

"The back door was open," I say. "And there are men's footprints on the kitchen floor. Who was here?"

"It was me," she whispers with a mischievous grin. "I wanted some air, so I opened the door."

I place the glasses of water on the coffee table and step back to take her in. She looks so small and weak, but she also won't meet my eye. "What about the footprints? Who was that?"

"I had a taxi driver bring me home. A nice man. He helped into the house."

"Through the back door?"

"Yes, dear. He dropped me off down the bottom of the next street and we walked down the back alley. A lot of people do it that way, it's easier access for cars coming from town."

"I see." I cross my arms. This could be the truth, I don't know. I'm ready to quiz Peggy some more when she rotates her head and looks me dead in the eyes.

"Can you put the television on, dear?"

The mundanity of the request and Peggy's soft voice throw me a little. I splutter something in the affirmative and grab the remote control from the coffee table. It takes me a few goes before I get it to work and some brightly lit studio game show flashes up on the screen.

"Ah, I like this one," Peggy says, wagging her finger at the screen. "This presenter fellow is a real hoot."

I turn and watch it with her. I've never been a big fan of television, so I've never seen this show before. It appears to be called The Chase and doesn't seem as banal as some of the stuff they schedule at this time of day. The sound from the television set clashes with the oppressive silence I've grown used to in this house but I'm not sure this way is any better.

"Do you ever get any of the questions right?" I ask, trying to ease the tension in the room.

When Peggy doesn't answer I turn back and see her eyes are closed and she's making the same purring noise she made last night. I look at the clock on the fireplace. It's only 6:00 p.m. but I suppose half a bottle of vodka will knock out even a seasoned drinker of Peggy's size. And this works out well for me. It means I can chill in the kitchen for a while in peace rather than go straight to my room. I'll make myself a cup of tea and go over some of my notes and the assignments on my laptop. I switch off the television and am about to tiptoe out of the room when Peggy sits up.

"What's going on?"

"Hey, it's okay," I whisper, patting the air with my hands. "You go back to sleep. Rest is good."

She stares past me into the hallway. "It's a sad old business," she says.

I can't help but follow her gaze. There's nothing there. "What is?"

"You know. All this…mess. It makes me sad."

I give her a reassuring smile. "Yes. But as you say, he'll be home tomorrow. Don't worry."

"Who will?"

I frown. "Ron. Your husband."

She closes her eyes again and lets out a deep sigh. "Ah yes. My Ron. And Charlotte is coming home too," she mumbles to herself as she drifts off. "It'll be fine once Charlotte gets here. She'll know what to do." I watch her for a few moments until I'm certain she's asleep then leave the room and close the door.

Oh yes. Sure. Charlotte's coming home. Charlotte, who sleeps in a single bed and has posters of a teenage Justin Timberlake on her wall. Charlotte who is either twenty-eight or thirty-four but who hasn't had a photo taken in nearly twenty years. That Charlotte is coming home, is she? I don't think so, dear. The more I think about it, the more I'm certain. Charlotte is dead. And poor Peggy is more broken and confused than I first thought.

TWENTY-FOUR

I wander into the kitchen and fill up the kettle. I've not had a hot drink since this morning's break and a cup of tea seems like a good plan. While I wait for the water to boil, I poke around in the cupboards and drawers, rummaging about somewhat carelessly. If anyone were to catch me, they'd likely think my actions were due to boredom or impatience rather than nosiness. But after a few minutes of snooping without any luck, I decide to try again in a more organized way, methodically going through every drawer one by one. The guilt of breaking Peggy's trust weighs heavily on me but I'm driven by an intense curiosity. The more time I spend in this house, the more troubled and confused Peggy seems; drunk one minute and talking of Charlotte's imminent return the next. She seems to believe her daughter is coming back soon and I seriously doubt that's possible.

So, I pull out drawers, I lift things out, I look under things and behind things, then I place it all back as I found it and slide the drawers shut. I have to find the truth of what happened to Charlotte. Maybe if I know what happened I can help Peggy somehow. I know from experience how dismissive and unhelpful social services can be. I need a cast iron story so I can demonstrate to them how vulnerable Peggy and Ron are and that they have – at the very least - memory issues. That way I might be able to get them the support they need. But I can't report anything with just my theory to go off.

I also know I'm doing this partly for myself. I need to know my instincts are correct and I'm not some paranoid loon.

The three drawers are mainly full of junk – old pens with the ends chewed-up, sewing kits, tattered bills and bank letters that should have been thrown out years ago. Frustrated, but not deterred, I move over to the free-standing drawer unit next to the fridge and pull open the top section.

Now, this is interesting. Sitting on top of another pile of old bills is a cardboard box. It's shallow in depth, which is why it fits in the drawer, but big enough for a letter or a large photo to fit inside. I carry it over to the table and place it down before lifting off the lid.

The first thing I see is a photo. Another one of Charlotte. In this one, she's about twelve and is standing with Peggy and Ron on a sea front somewhere. They're all holding ice creams and Charlotte is grinning manically at the camera. Her hair is white-blonde, and her parents are both gazing at her with their expressions full of love and affection. And it's the right sort of love, too. Parental, caring, protective. I don't know why I can tell all that from a photo but that's how it makes me feel. I lift out the photo and place it on the table before turning my attention to the other documents in the box. I find an old mortgage deed made out to Ronald and Margaret Clifton in 1984, a couple of paper tv licences and then...

"Oh, bloody hell," I mutter to myself as I lift out a letter from Merseyside Police, along with a court summons for a

Miss Charlotte Elizabeth Clifton and then a coroner's report. It looks very official and with the adrenaline now lighting up my system it's hard for me to focus on any one section, but I notice Charlotte's name and the words *Accidental Death* written at the top of the page.

I was right.

Charlotte is dead.

I feel dizzy suddenly but hold myself together enough to scan down the rest of the document. Halfway down it says, 'Medical Death: Immediate Course of Death' and then the words, 'Combined Heroin and Alcohol Toxicity'.

I read on, flitting from document to document until I've got the whole picture. It turns out Charlotte died six years ago, when she was twenty-eight, my age. That means she would have been thirty-four if she was alive so I suppose Peggy and Ron were both sort of correct when they told me her age. Those poor people. As I read on, I see her address is listed as somewhere in Liverpool and that she'd been living there for over ten years. I see no mention of any nursing degree. I wonder if that was what she'd planned on doing with her life – and had talked to her parents about doing - before circumstances took her down a very different path.

A sound from the front room startles me and I quickly place all the papers back in the box and the photo on top the way I found it. Then I put the box back in the drawer and slide it shut. Once done, I stand still and listen but there's no more noise.

I feel so desperately sad for Peggy. But discovering the truth about Charlotte doesn't change anything. In fact, it only troubles me more. Is this something I really want to get involved with?

I have a tendency, especially when I'm depressed, to

meddle in other people's business. It's a self-defence mechanism, I suppose. A way of deflecting my attention away from my own problems.

Is that what I'm doing here?

Regardless, I'm not sure if I should be getting involved with the Cliftons' welfare. After all, I'm only staying in their spare room. Even if I was related and wanted to help, what do I expect to happen? I imagine myself calling social services to report my concerns about two old people who can't accept their daughter is dead. I know just how badly that would go.

Yet I feel compelled to do something. Too many people have turned their backs on me over the years. Even though I now know the truth about Charlotte I still have heaps of unanswered questions. Like, whose footprints do I keep seeing in the backyard and whose voice did I hear the other night? Was it Pete? Was it part of my dream? Or was it someone else entirely?

Steam pours from the kettle as the water inside comes to a boil but I leave it. Tea will have to wait. I have to find out what's going on in this house. And I think I know where to look.

TWENTY-FIVE

I look in on Peggy in the front room. She's fast asleep and snoring so I continue down the hallway and head upstairs. As I climb, I check my phone. It's a few minutes after nine but the weariness I felt earlier has vanished. My entire being bristles with nervous energy as I reach the landing and walk over to Charlotte's old bedroom. The padlock is still missing, and I unhook the metal plate from the clasp and ease open the door. It smells musty in the room; more so than I remember from the last time I was here. But maybe because I'm now experiencing the space with the knowledge that this is the room of a dead girl.

One thing still bothers me. Why did she leave home so young? It dawns on me that maybe it was to study like Peggy said. If Charlotte was eighteen when she left, rather than sixteen, it would make more sense. Have I been mis-ageing the photos I've seen of her? People do look younger than they are sometimes. I go to the old desk unit standing next to the bed. The chair creaks as I sit down to take it all in. A desk tidy sits in one corner of the desk, complete with pens and paper clips.

A large ball of blue-tac and a rainbow-coloured eraser sit beside this, along with a stack of old notepads and loose papers. Everything is covered in a layer of dust. I blow some of it away and riffle through the papers and notepads but don't find anything of any interest. One of the notepads is an old schoolbook of Charlotte's with the word 'News' written on the front. Inside it appears to be a sort of diary where the pre-teen Charlotte – my guess would be she's about ten - has written about what she did the previous weekend. I read a few of the entries.

In the first one, she talks about going to visit her mum's friend and playing in the garden with some ducks. In another entry, she and her mum and dad go to a museum and have lunch at a local pub. It sounds like she had a nice life and that the three of them had a nice life together. My heart breaks the more I read. I close the book and put it back on the pile.

What went wrong, I wonder, for Charlotte to end her life at the other end of a needle?

My best guess is she got in with a bad crowd and after clashes with her parents, she left home sometime between sixteen and eighteen. Peggy and Ron no doubt held out hope she'd see sense and return to them, even going so far as to leave her bedroom set out exactly as she left it. But she never came home. And now her old room is a shrine to the girl she was before life and heroin took her away from them forever. A lot of the girls I grew up with in the care system got into heroin. I was lucky. Because of how my mum was I turned away from anything I felt was destructive or too personality-altering. But I never blamed anyone for getting into that world, it's an easy path to start down and a hard one to leave. And, from what I gather, it takes you away from your problems and makes you feel good about yourself. Who wouldn't want that?

The desk has three drawers down one side and I slide the first one open. Inside is a selection of old newspaper clippings and certificates. I lift out the top few pieces, the first is a photograph, cut out from a local newspaper. The print is faded and the paper is so yellow and thin that I'm worried it will disintegrate in my hands. The picture shows a group of children dressed in their school uniform all giving big grins to the camera whilst a woman in ceremonial dress stands beside them. Most of the children are missing teeth and the caption below reads: 'Market Allerton Primary School Class 6 welcomes Mayor Anderson to the school.' I peer at the children's faces but can't pick out Charlotte. But she's there I imagine, looking out at me through time.

The rest of the papers are certificates and awards that Charlotte acquired over her time at school and elsewhere. There's one for swimming a length of a pool using breaststroke, one for cycling proficiency, another says 'Class member of the month.' I realise I'm smiling to myself as I flick through the pile. Like a proud parent might. I almost feel as if I know Charlotte by now. It's such a sad tale. No parent should ever have to bury their child.

What?

I hear something behind me and glance over my shoulder to check. The room is empty and, so far as I can see, so is the landing. Regardless, I get up off the chair and wander out of the room, fists balled and ready.

"Hello?" I whisper, at the doorway. "Who's there?"

I step out onto the landing. The area is still and quiet. No one else is around. The door to my room is open a few inches, however, and I don't remember leaving it open when I left this morning. I also didn't notice it was open when I passed by on the way to Charlotte's room a few minutes earlier. I tread over to it, snaking my hand around the side of the door and switching on the light as I simultaneously open the door.

I hiss as the room flashes into light, an attempt to appear braver than I am. But the room is empty. I look around. One of the bottles of water has been replenished but apart from that everything is how I left it. I shake my head. My heart is beating faster than ever and my stomach muscles ache with tension.

"Calm yourself, Lauren," I mutter to myself. "You're letting this get out of hand."

I turn around and step back onto the landing. I remain there for a few seconds and listen. I hear sounds from under the floorboards which are probably the pipes rattling as the central heating comes on. Was that what I heard? Probably. It's amazing how the mind can distort the most innocent events when it's already in a heightened state of stress.

I wait for another second or two and then go back into Charlotte's room. Now I feel even more ridiculous and vile being here. Am I one of those sick goons who turn up at the site of a murder – who think because they've listened to a couple of real crime podcasts that they're better equipped to solve the case than the police? It's also pointless for me to be in here. It's clear this room holds no clues regarding Charlotte's death or why Peggy and Ron have chosen to preserve it in this way.

I replace the certificates in the drawer and slide it shut, before placing the chair under the desk the way I found it. I turn around and am about to leave when my eyes fall on the wardrobe. I've already looked inside but one more check won't hurt, will it? Then I'll leave this room and Charlotte's memory alone, satisfied there is nothing here that points to anything but old memories and regret.

I stand in front of the wardrobe and pull open the doors to be met with the two dresses I've already seen hanging inside. I check the base of the unit but there's nothing there. I check the shelf above the main clothes rail and find an old shoe box. As I lift it down a fresh wave of adrenaline ripples down my back but, on lifting the lid, I find a pair of old ballet pumps. Nothing else.

Okay, time to leave the poor girl alone now!

I place the shoe box back and am heading for the door when my foot kicks against something. I look down to see whatever it is rolling across the carpet. It's a cylindrical object about three inches long and my first thought is it's an old marker pen or maybe a large battery. However, as I lean down to pick it up, I see I'm wrong. My breath catches in my throat as I hold it up in front of me. It's a roll of twenty-pound notes, fastened with a red rubber band. I turn the money around in my hand, inspecting the thickness of the wad. There has to be at least three thousand pounds in the roll.

And as I stare down at it I can't help thinking that things have just got a whole lot more serious.

TWENTY-SIX

I switch out the light and close the door and then hurry across the landing to the spare room. Once inside and, with the door locked, I sit on the bed, holding the roll of twenty-pound notes in my lap. I've never seen this much money before, never mind held it. The roll is tightly wound but doesn't weigh as much as I imagined it would. I yank off the rubber band and open out the roll. I need to see exactly what I'm dealing with.

It takes me a minute to count the notes. There are actually ninety-eight twenties in total which makes it considerably less than three-thousand pounds. Okay, so maths was never my strong point, but I work out there's one-thousand, nine-hundred and sixty pounds in total. That strikes me as odd. It would make more sense for it to be an even two thousand and I have to stop my busy mind from racing into histrionic scenarios – picturing shadowy gangsters peeling two twenties off the roll to offer as an incentive or a bribe.

But it's not just my overactive imagination at play. The fact remains, Peggy and Ron have left the best part of two-thousand pounds on the floor in their dead daughter's bedroom. I'd say most people would be curious as to where it came from. This house is becoming more disconcerting by the day.

Then I remember...

The disappearing hold-alls. The shadowy men in the back-yard in the early hours of the morning. These things have to be linked somehow. I roll my shoulders back and fill my lungs with air to compose myself. I need a clear mind. I need to think this through logically.

The only rational explanation I come up with is that the Cliftons are being taken advantage of somehow. I've heard about this before. Gangsters prey on vulnerable people and use their houses to stash drugs or stolen goods. Or money. What is it they call it? Cuckooing? The term deriving, I imagine, from the way cuckoos lay their eggs in other birds' nests and take them over. Some shitty criminal has seen these two damaged, defenceless souls and decided they're fair game.

I think about the back door always left open and the foot-prints I saw and all at once I realise I might be in more danger than I ever imagined. But why would these people allow the Cliftons to rent out their spare room if they were using the place as a stash house? It doesn't make sense. But none of this makes sense. I roll the money up and secure the roll with the rubber band. I feel more exposed and isolated than I have done for some time, but I'm also angry. Angry at life, angry that there are people in the world who would take advantage of Peggy. And angry at myself for getting involved. But here I am. I can't stop now. I need to know the truth.

I shove the money roll in my pocket and leave my room. I have to speak to Peggy. Up to this point, she's not been the most reliable of people, but if strange men are coming in and out of her house, she must know about it.

I go downstairs and through into the front room. Peggy's chair is empty. I head down the hallway and find her pottering around in the kitchen. I stand in the doorway and watch as she takes a loaf of bread out of the cupboard and places it on the worktop before going to the fridge and removing a tub of butter. To look at her you wouldn't guess she was asleep only a few minutes earlier. Her actions are erratic and nervy.

"Peggy?" I say, softly. "What are you doing?"

She looks at me but doesn't stop as she carries the butter over to the worktop. "I'm making sandwiches," she says. "I thought you might want something to eat."

I walk around the table as she busies herself buttering the bread. I lean against the worktop to try to make eye contact but she doesn't look up.

"You don't have to do that," I tell her. She butters one side of the bread and then turns it over and starts buttering the other side. "Peggy, you're getting it all over the worktop. Come here." I reach out and take the knife from her. It's only a butter knife and would do no damage to anyone but I need her to focus.

She does a strange shivering motion and then looks at me. Now she's smiling and happy again, back to a facsimile of Nana Mary. Her face lights up the way it did when I first saw her on the doorstep.

"Aren't you pretty." She reaches for my face. At first, I flinch but then allow her to stroke my cheek with her cold, bony fingers. "Such a good face. Just like my Charlotte."

I force a smile. "Thank you. She was very beautiful. I bet you miss her a lot."

"She's a very good girl," she says, not picking up on my use of the past tense. Whether this is down to habit, delusion or both I'm not sure. Her eyes give nothing away. "I think you're going to get on really well, the two of you," she adds.

Okay. That's not right.

The way she giggles after saying this, almost like a child herself, crushes me. Either she actually believes Charlotte is alive or she's so desperate for her to be she'd rather pretend she was than face reality. I don't want to push the matter any further. Not now, at least. There are bigger and more disturbing issues I want to get to the bottom of first.

"Can we sit down a minute?" I ask. Peggy seems flustered at this request and mumbles something about the sandwiches. I take her hand and lead her over to the table. "Please sit. I have a few questions I need to ask you."

Peggy tuts but does as I request. I take the seat beside her and turn my chair around so I'm facing her.

"I found this upstairs," I say, pulling the money roll out of my pocket. "Is it yours?"

Peggy's eyes widen at the bound twenties in my hand. "Where did you get that from?"

That wasn't the response I was expecting. Nor was I expecting her to snatch the money roll from out of my hand. "Oh...Peggy..." I gasp as she grabs it and clutches it to her chest. "Sorry. I didn't realise—"

"This is my money," she snaps. "I need it. Where did you find it?"

"It was upstairs," I say. "On the landing." I don't want to tell her I was in Charlotte's room, but the grim irony of this fact doesn't escape me. Because I'm lying to the poor woman as well. Taking advantage of her confused state.

"Thank you for retrieving it," she says, still holding it tight against her. She grabs the edge of the table with the other hand and gets to her feet. "I'll just put it here for safekeeping." She waddles over to the worktop and puts it in the corner behind the kettle and next to the fridge.

When she turns around, she's not smiling the way she normally does. She looks like she's seen a ghost.

"You can talk to me," I tell her, nodding at the same time. "If something is bothering you if some*one* is bothering you, then I can help."

"Bothering me?" She returns to her seat at the table but doesn't look at me. Instead, she stares down into her quivering rheumatic hands.

I try again. "Listen to me, Peggy. I think someone is coming into your house. Someone you don't like being here. Am I right?" She lifts her head slightly but not enough so I can see her face. Her shoulders shudder. "If you talk to me about it, I can help you. You don't have to live like this."

"It's just me and Ron. And Charlotte," she says, before releasing the hint of a laugh. "And you, of course."

I swallow, fighting the people pleaser inside of me who wants to accept this explanation and not make the old woman feel any more uncomfortable. "I think there are other people, too," I say. "Has anyone ever threatened you or Ron?"

"No, dear."

"Did someone hurt Ron? Is that what happened?"

"No, dear." She shakes her head.

A prickle of frustration tightens my chest, followed by a sinking feeling in my belly. But I know what I have to ask next.

"Do you know a man called Pete?" I ask. "He lives on this street, a few doors down."

Peggy sniffs. "Pete? No."

"Pete, or Peter. He's quite tall with short brown hair." I could say he's got a nice smile and kind eyes but who knows if that's true. I would have said the same about Graham – a man who I believed I'd be with forever - and I didn't know him at all.

Peggy shakes her head. "No, dear." She raises her head a little more. "Please stop asking me these questions. I don't like it. It's not very nice."

"I'm sorry," I tell her. "But I'm worried about you. I think something is going on in this house and it's not right. I want to help you."

"Everything is fine. Everything is lovely. Please stop."

She looks up and as I stare into her watery eyes, I sense real fear in them. What's causing her to feel this way I'm not certain – Ron being in the hospital, her own depleting mind, or something more sinister – but I've enough experience of this terrible world to know when someone is genuinely scared. And it's written all over Peggy's face.

TWENTY-SEVEN

I squeeze Peggy's hand. I need her to be strong. I need her to find the courage to tell me exactly what is going on in this house. As I stare into her eyes I think she's going to crack but then she looks away and chuckles and it's like the last five minutes haven't happened. After stating once more that 'everything is lovely' she's back to being the vague but friendly old woman I met three nights earlier. Yet, I'm certain I saw a hint of the real Peggy just now. There was something in her eyes that told me she knew more than she was letting on. She was lucid, even if it was only for a brief moment.

She tells me she wants to go back into the front room, and I help her down the hallway and into her armchair.

"Will you stay here with me?" she asks, once she's settled.

The clock on the mantlepiece tells me it's almost ten. I have another early start tomorrow, but I suppose another half hour won't matter. Plus, I'm still harbouring the belief Peggy has more to say. If I stay with her and gain more of her trust, maybe she'll open up to me.

But as I make myself comfortable on the side of the sofa

nearest her chair, I quickly realise this is not going to happen. It's as if she's already slipped back into the past. She talks about Ron and their marriage and how he used to buy her flowers every Friday on his way home from work. I understand that these memories are a refuge for her, a safe place to inhabit away from the cruelty of life, but inside I'm frustrated as hell. When she tells me about how Ron and she bought their house in 1976 for just four-thousand pounds I smile and nod and make the appropriate noises before clearing my throat and asking her if she feels safe here.

When she doesn't answer I try again. "Is anyone coming into this house that you don't want to be here, Peggy?"

She scowls and looks out of the window. I don't dare breathe in case she's about to say something important. But then she shrugs and tells me once more that she's fine. *All* is fine. She says it with such an assured tone that I wonder if I've got it wrong. Because maybe she is fine. Maybe it's me who's confused. Maybe I'm still looking for drama where there isn't any to distract me from my own problems.

I don't know what to do for the best. I've always been cautious of the police and social services and, even if I did bite the bullet and call them, what would I say? All the evidence I have to back up my wild theory regarding people taking advantage of the old couple is an open back door, some footprints, and a roll of money. I'm not sure it'd stand up in court, as they say. More than likely, the police would fob me off like they always do. The same with social services.

Plus, there could be an innocent explanation for the money. Maybe Peggy and Ron keep their savings in Charlotte's room. That would explain the lock on the door. I've heard of people hoarding their money because they don't trust banks. I look at Peggy as she stares out the window, looking at something only she can see. I want to ask her some more about the money, but I don't want to stress her out any more than I have to. She seems to like me, but she doesn't know me well. If the money is hers and there's more stored in the house, I could really freak her out by going on about it.

I lean back and rest my head on the sofa cushion. Maybe this is all in my head. Peggy says the money is hers and who am I to doubt her? It wouldn't be the first time I've jumped too quickly to conclusions.

I puff out my cheeks. It's time to leave this alone. It's making me anxious and that's the last thing I need. This week was supposed to be the start of me turning my life around. I was here to get my qualification and enjoy some much-needed downtime in the evenings. It's funny how life works out.

If you don't laugh, you'll cry…

I lean forward and slap my hands on my thighs, the way people do when they want others to know they're ready to leave. When Peggy looks over, I raise my eyebrows, about to tell her I'm going up to bed.

"There you are," she says. "How are you, my darling?"

She laughs and for once I'm lost for words. "Excuse me?"

"Are you well?" she says, tilting her head to one side. "Do you need anything?"

I narrow my eyes at her, trying to work out where she's coming from. Is this Peggy in her night-time haze or is it something else? I chew on my lip, considering if I should say what's on my mind. It could seem cruel but it might help Peggy in the long run. I glance at the clock. It's getting late and I might not get another chance.

"Do you think I'm Charlotte, Peggy?" I say, lowering my chin.

She scoffs. "Yes. Charlotte. My Charlotte."

"No. I'm not her, Peggy. My name's Lauren. I'm staying in your spare room for a few nights, that's all." I smile at her and wait for a response, but she turns back to the window. I take a deep breath and go for it. "Peggy, is Charlotte…dead?"

As soon as I say it, I'm overcome with dizziness. I fight through it and shift forward onto the edge of the sofa as I wait for the question to land. At first, I wonder if Peggy hasn't heard me but then her mouth trembles and it's like all the life-force has been sucked out of her. I want to go to her, to comfort her. But I don't. She stares off into the middle distance and looks as if she's about to burst into tears. A second goes by. And then another. The room is so quiet it's oppressive. When it becomes apparent that tears aren't going to materialise and she's not going to reply, I lean forward, so I can look her in the eyes.

"Peggy?"

She shudders. "What is it dear?"

"Charlotte. I was asking you what happened to her?"

She giggles. "You're Charlotte."

"No. I'm not. I'm Lauren."

"Ah, yes." She nods and holds up a crooked finger. "You're a good girl. Like my Charlotte. She looks after Ron and me."

I let out another long sigh. It's so sad to hear the old woman talk like this. She's lost everything and I know what that feels like. I decide to let the moment settle and lift my necklace out of my jumper. As I often do in times of stress, I roll the locket pendant around in my fingers. It's empty but contains more sentiment than it could ever hold. This was my mum's necklace. It's the only thing of hers I have left, the only thing she ever gave me. Unless you count the cigarette burns on my arms. Over the years I've tried to piece together the vague memories I have of that time, but most of my experience of my mother comes from what I've learnt from others. I don't remember living with her, for instance, which means I don't consciously remember the abuse or pushing her down the stairs. I do remember a lot of shouting and the flashing lights of the ambulance and police cars but that's all. My first real memory of my mum is actually the lack of her. Which was hard when I was younger and didn't understand why I didn't have a family like other kids. But now I believe it was better in the long run. It meant I never pined for her. Instead, most of my energy was taken up trying to work out who I was in the world without having anyone there to guide me. I'm not sure I've figured it out yet, but I think my troubled childhood is the reason I always root for the underdog or spend my time yearning for a normality that never even existed. It's been said by more than one therapist that I look out at the world through rose-tinted spectacles. This may be so, but mine are nowhere near as strong as Peggy's.

"Charlotte is coming here tomorrow," she says as if to highlight this fact. "You can meet her."

"She's coming here? Tomorrow?" I repeat, unsure if I should play along or not. "And will she be staying over?"

"I don't think so."

"I see. When was the last time she visited?"

Peggy looks right at me and this time I see nothing but joy in her eyes. "It was a few weeks ago. We played cards. She used to love playing cards with me and her dad."

The poor deluded old woman. But who wouldn't pretend their life was better if they could get away with the lie? Especially at her age. I worry suddenly that I'm doing her a disservice by getting involved in her business.

What if she's happy in her haziness?

What if this is what she wants?

For some reason, Graham pops into my mind. But it doesn't take much. He knew I wanted a better life, and that fitted in well with his knight-on-a-white horse complex.

Here comes the big brave hero, to save the broken damsel from a life worse than death.

The problem was as soon as I started to feel confident and stronger-willed, he lost interest. Thinking about it now I can pinpoint the exact moment he started to tire of me. It was when I got the job at Briars. Suddenly I was independent. I had my mojo back. I didn't need him as much as I had done. I thought that was a good thing. I thought it was what he wanted for me.

But no.

What a total dick head.

He probably only proposed to me because he wanted to feel like the big man again. My protector. But in the end, that didn't satisfy his fantasy either.

Perhaps I'm being overly harsh, but it helps me to think this way. Being around truly broken people like Peggy puts my problems into perspective. I look over at her. Her eyes are closed and she looks so peaceful.

Too peaceful?

I get up and go over to her, my heart pounding in my chest as I scan her body for signs that she's alive.

Thankfully, as I lean in close, I hear the gentle wheeze of her breathing and then she mutters something I can't make out.

Hell, Peggy. You had me going for a minute.

Letting my shoulders drop, I watch her for a moment before leaving the room and going back through to the kitchen. A reflex stronger than reason carries me over to the cupboard where I stashed the bottle of vodka.

I carry it over to the table, grabbing a glass from the draining board on my way and pouring myself a healthy measure. I rarely drink spirits and definitely not neat, but I feel as if I need a large one.

I down the vodka in one go. It tastes foul but I enjoy the burn in my throat. It makes me feel hard. I pour myself another and hold it up as if toasting the universe.

Here's to Lauren Williams.

I drink this back in one gulp and slam the glass down on the table. As I sit back, I cast my gaze around the kitchen, taking in the dirty lino on the floor, the old units, the fridge that was no doubt once white but is now the same dirty magnolia colour as the walls and ceiling. Then I think of the photos on the Samstone Manor website. It could have been so different.

But I've only got two more nights here and... *No!*

I can't do it.

Right now, I have a fire in me and I need to stoke it, to keep it going. If I stay any longer in this weird house full of sadness, it's going to sap my renewed sense of purpose. It will drag me down.

I place the glass on the table, already knowing what I have to do. What I'm going to do. Tonight will be the last night I stay here. If I have to use my credit card to book a hellishly expensive room elsewhere, then so be it. I'll be able to pay it off in a few months. I've got a new job now. I deserve one night of luxury after the stresses and strains of this week.

I replace the bottle of vodka in the cupboard and rinse out the glass before placing it back where I found it next to the sink. Once I'm out of this place and with more perspective, I'll reconsider whether I report what I've seen here. I could do it as an anonymous tip-off if I don't want to get involved. Then, whatever is going on here is in the hands of the police or social services.

I leave the kitchen and walk down the hallway, stopping outside the front room where Peggy is sleeping soundly in her armchair. Can I do it to her? I suspect if the authorities ever got around to completing a risk assessment review on Peggy and Ron's situation they'd find them too vulnerable to support themselves. Would they then take them into a home? Would they split them up? I don't expect so, but knowing what I know about social services I wouldn't be surprised if it happened. I knew a girl, Priya, who was split up from two of her brothers and had no idea where they were. She was only twelve.

I leave Peggy to her slumber. I wonder if she's dreaming about Charlotte and Ron and ice creams on the beach. A time when she was happy. When life was still full of joy and possibility. On my way upstairs I check the front door. It's locked, as usual, but for once I'm glad of this fact. I slide the deadbolts home and jiggle the door handle to make sure it's secure. No one is coming through that door tonight and tomorrow I'll be gone.

I grab the banister and haul myself up the stairs to the spare room. I don't look at Charlotte's room as I pass by. Not interested. I just want to get out of this house and forget I was ever here. Peggy is a nice lady but I don't know her. She's not Nana Mary. She's not my family. And one thing I've learnt over the years is you can't save everyone. I should have trusted my instincts on day one. And it's awful to say it but whatever is going on in this house, it isn't my responsibility or my problem. I can't fight everyone's battles.

Hell, I can barely fight my own.

TWENTY-EIGHT

I sit upright in bed and switch off my phone on the first beep of my alarm. Sunlight filters through the curtains and, as my awareness spreads and my memory clicks online, I'm reminded of the decisions I made last night. To not only leave Peggy's house and book into a hotel for my last night in town but to delete Graham's number and move on with my life.

I'm done feeling sorry for myself. I'm done tolerating shitty situations and allowing life to happen to me. Today I'm taking back control and that starts with getting out of this spare room and into a nice hotel, where I can relax and enjoy a long soak in a hot bath. It's been so very long since I allowed myself a bit of pampering. I think I damn well deserve it.

But first I have to follow through with my decision. I grab my phone and scroll through my contact list to find Graham's number. But as my finger hovers over the delete button I stop. What if I need to contact him for some reason? What if I realise, I've left something important at his house and I need to pick it up?

I let out a low groan, angry at myself I can't even carry out this simple act of self-care. I *will* delete his number, I promise myself. Just not yet. And that doesn't mean I can't follow through on the second part of my plan. Closing the contacts list, I open up the booking site I found the other day and leave the sluggish internet connection to load up while I get ready for my course.

I grab a towel, my toilet bag and some smart clothes for the day ahead and hurry across the landing to the bathroom. Once there I switch on the shower and undress while the water warms up. Being here in this cold bathroom, with its dusty pipes and ageing porcelain only strengthens my resolve to get out of this place. As I clamber over the side of the bath and under the water, I picture myself laying back in a deep, free-standing bathtub, as the subdued mood lighting reflects off the gold taps and marble tiles.

Yes. That'll do nicely.

I wash and dry myself before cleaning my teeth and applying a little foundation and mascara. I used to wear full make-up every day, but I've got out of the habit lately. I could probably pinpoint the moment when that happened, but I'm not thinking about that period of my life anymore. I'm not thinking about that dickhead.

I get dressed and inspect myself in the full-length mirror next to the door. I'm delighted to see I look brighter-eyed and fresher-faced than I have done in weeks. This, after two large glasses of neat vodka as well. It just goes to show, a positive attitude trumps a hangover any day of the week.

When I get back to my room, I check my phone and see the broker website has now loaded. I don't trust the slow internet to allow me to book online but my phone's location services mean the front page shows hotels in the surrounding area and there are phone numbers next to each listing. I scroll down the list and pick the third option, which is the second cheapest hotel but still comes in at two-hundred and thirty-eight pounds for the night. It's a lot of money but screw it. It's worth it.

I'm worth it.

I call the number and speak with a woman with a strong accent who could be Polish. She's pleasant and helpful and I book a double room with an en suite bathroom and even opt for the breakfast option for tomorrow morning. It's only another fifteen pounds and after a week of mainly cold sand-wiches and toast a decent feed is just what I need.

I tell the woman I'll see her later and hang up to wait for the confirmation email to tell me I'm booked in. When it even-tually arrives a shiver of excitement runs through me. It's done. No going back. For one night, the boutique Gilded Griffin Hotel will be my haven. My glorious palace away from the outside world. I'm not sure how work would react if they knew I was leaving my accommodation a day early, but there's no reason why they would find out. Besides if I explained the situation, I'm sure they wouldn't view my leaving Peggy's place as me being ungrateful or unprofessional. All I want is one night of luxury. One night, where I don't have to deal with strange men outside my window or the spectre of poor Char-lotte Clifton looming at me from every wall.

I close down my emails and see the time on my phone's home screen.

Bugger.

Now I'm running late. I pick up my suitcase and chuck it on the bed before grabbing my clothes out of the wardrobe and stuffing them inside. I don't bother folding anything, I haven't time. Once my clothes are packed, I unzip the document compartment and check my passport is still in there. I didn't need it in the end, but I might this evening when I check into the Gilded Griffin. I also plan on using it a lot this year, once I've done a few months at GP Telecom and can start booking holidays. I'm going to travel a lot. Wherever I can get to. I'm young, I'm free and I'm single, and very soon I'll have a decent job with a decent income. Nothing can stop me.

Feeling more determined than ever I close my suitcase and carry it downstairs. Clinking noises coming from the kitchen tell me Peggy is already up, so I leave my bags by the front door and walk down the hallway to say goodbye. There's no reason for me to tell her the truth about why I'm leaving a day early. I'll tell her something has come up at work.

I'm up in my head, mentally rehearsing what I'm going to say to her, so when I walk into the kitchen and see Ron sitting at the table it takes a few seconds for it to sink in.

"Look who's here," Peggy says, on seeing me. "My Ron. He's come home to me!"I smile and nod and try to get my words out. "Yes. I can see." I tilt my head to look at Ron. "How are you feeling?"

He stares at me with wide, unblinking eyes. "I'm all right, girl. Thank you.

"When did he get back?" I ask Peggy, lowering my voice so Ron won't hear me.

She leans back. "Late last night. I think. Did you not hear him come home?"

"No. I was in bed."

"Right. Yes."

"How did he get here?"

Peggy frowns. "Umm...someone from the hospital brought him. Is that what happened, Ron? A man from the hospital?"

She sounds vague and unsure of herself but as her eyes land on Ron's face she smiles. "It's so good to have him home."

I smile over gritted teeth. I know I should leave this alone, but I can't help myself. "Sorry," I say. "Who brought him home?"

Ron sniffs. "A man. A friend of ours."

I keep my eyes on Peggy as he says this, but she doesn't flinch. "Right. I see." So, not someone from the hospital? I want to delve deeper, but I stop myself. Last night I made a decision, and I will stick to it.

This is not my problem.

I can't save everyone.

"Charlotte is coming around to see us later, as well," Peggy says, still beaming.

"Oh? Is she?"

"Yes. She'll make everything all right again. Won't she, Ron?"

Ron grins. "Aye. She will that."

Once again, I'm compelled to ask more questions but I'm already running late. Plus, my luxury hotel is booked and I just need to get the hell out of here.

"Well, I hope you have a nice evening and I'm glad you're on the mend, Mr Clifton." I glance at Peggy. "Could you open the door for me, please? I need to leave, or I'll be late for my bus."

"Yes, of course." She waddles around the table and I step aside to let her pass. As she walks down the hallway, I give the kitchen one last glance and my eyes linger on the back door for a moment, before I turn and follow Peggy to the front door.

"Oh, are you leaving?" she asks, gesturing to my suitcase.

"Yes. It's a shame. I have to go back to Manchester straight after the course tonight," I'm hoping my tone sounds as matter of fact as I intend it to. "You see, I was mistaken. I thought it was a five-day course, but it was only four days. Silly me." I roll my eyes. I'm not sure I sound convincing, but I don't care.

"Well, it was nice to have you here, dear," Peggy says, sliding the deadbolts open. "You take care of yourself now, won't you?"

"I will. And you too, Peggy." I swallow. I want to say more – much more - but time is against me. I've got less than ten minutes to get to the bus stop. I turn to her. "You do know there are people who you can ring if you need help."

She closes her eyes and nods. "Yes. But I'm fine, dear. I've got everything I need." She produces a key from out of her pocket and with a shaking hand unlocks the door. She looks at me as she opens it and as the day's bright sun illuminates her face, she looks older and feebler than she's ever done. "You take care."

"I will. Thank you. And please stay safe. If anything – or any*one* – is upsetting you then you should call someone. The police, if you need to. They can help. Promise me you will?"

"I know, dear." For a split-second, I see something else behind her eyes. Gone is the benevolent mistiness and, in its place, a resigned knowing. I wonder, is Peggy another woman forced to tolerate the shitty situation she's found herself in? But what else can she do at her age? I want to reach out to her and pull her close. I want to protect her. But I don't and I can't. This isn't my battle.

"Thank you," I tell her. "For everything."

Then I grab my case and hurry down the street towards the bus stop. I'm free. At least one of us is.

TWENTY-NINE

The bus is already at the stop as I turn the corner. Tightening my grip on the handle of my suitcase I fall into a jog and then a run. This is the last bus that will get me to Samstone Manor in time for the first session. I can't miss it. I wave my free arm, shouting for it to wait as I pull my suitcase along behind me. I'm twenty yards away when I feel it pull over to one side and, as I turn back, I see it's flipped off its wheel and fallen into the road.

Shit!

Bloody hell!

I stop and flip the suitcase back on the pavement and onto its wheels. I don't need this. Not now. As I set off again, I wave my arm frantically to alert the driver. Whether he sees me or not is unclear, but I'm still a few yards away when the bus's bi-fold doors suck shut and it pulls away from the kerb.

"No! Please! Wait!" I catch up with it and bang on the side with my open palm. "I have to catch this!"

It's no use. I run alongside it for another few strides but it's not going to stop. I shake my fist helplessly at the bus as it picks up speed and disappears around the bend at the end of the street.

What am I going to do?

I check my phone. It's 8:45 a.m. My course starts in half an hour, but the next bus doesn't arrive until 9:20 a.m. I'm going to be late. I can't be late. I throw my attention up and down the street, searching the signs hanging above the shop fronts in the hope one of them says *Taxi*. I'm out of luck. If I ever had any to begin with. But there has to be a taxi firm somewhere in Market Allerton. I set off walking towards the centre of town when a car horn makes me jump.

What the…?

Are they beeping at me?

I look around, already riled and ready to give whoever it is a piece of my mind when a silver Audi pulls up beside me and I see Pete behind the wheel.

I lean over so I can look through the passenger window as he winds it down. "Did you miss the bus?" he asks.

"Yes! I ran for the bloody thing, but it wouldn't wait."

"What a nightmare. Some of those bus drivers are cut-throat. Do you want a lift?" He looks smarter than the last time I saw him and is wearing a maroon shirt with black tie and dark grey trousers.

I click my teeth as I consider his offer. He's a nice guy, I'm sure of it. Yet there is something about him that's not quite right.

"I don't want to put you out," I tell him. "I was going to walk down the main street and see if I can find a taxi."

He pulls a face like he's smelt something rotten. "You might be lucky. But at this time of day, I doubt it. If there are any about, they'll be picking up old dears from the local Tesco."

I stand up and give the street another once over. He makes a good point, and I don't relish the idea of lugging my suitcase around the streets looking for a ride. Plus, the longer I leave it the later I'm going to be for my course.

"Okay, if you're sure."

"Of course, let me give you a hand." He turns off the engine and leaps out to help me with my suitcase. I go to protest, but he's picked it up and shoved it onto the back seat before I have a chance. "Thanks," I say.

He grins. "No problem." I get the impression he's about to open the passenger door for me but thinks better of it. Instead, he waves his hand over it. "Get in."

I open the door and climb in and once he's restarted the engine we set off. I watch out the window as we leave the town behind and hit the countryside. Travelling in a car rather than a bus means I should get to Samstone Manor with plenty of time to spare. That thought lifts my spirits. I'll be able to grab a much-needed cup of coffee and a bite to eat before the course starts.

As we drive along Pete quizzes me more about the course and how I've found it staying with the Cliftons. No doubt he's only making conversation but I'm wary of answering his question so only give him as much as is polite, but no more. I tell him the same as I told Peggy. That the course finishes today so I'm heading straight back to Manchester afterwards

"I thought it was for five days and you were staying until Friday," he says.

I snap my head to look at him. I don't remember telling him that but maybe I did. I was a bit tipsy that night in the pub "Actually the truth is I needed to get out of that house," I tell him, laughing to cover my embarrassment. "I'm staying elsewhere tonight. At The Gilded Griffin. Do you know it?"

"I've heard of it," he says and sticks out his bottom lip. "It's supposed to be very nice."

I puff out my cheeks. "That's what I'm hoping for. It can't be any worse than that place."

He frowns. "Did something bad happen?" he asks, and there's something in his tone of voice that I don't like. He sounds too eager.

"No. Not really. I fancied a bit of luxury for my last night, that's all."

"Right. Sure. I only ask because last time we met you said something about some weird goings-on. Did you get to the bottom of it?"

I tense. It'd be good to get another person's perspective on all that has happened, but my guts are telling me to keep quiet. Even if Pete is a completely innocent party, it's not fair to speculate, especially with him being Peggy and Ron's neighbour.

If in doubt, don't trust anyone.

That should be my new mantra for a while.

As we continue on our way, I watch Pete out of the corner of my eye. Indeed, he doesn't seem the type to be involved in anything sinister. But what type of person would he have to be to take advantage of two broken-hearted pensioners?

"Have you ever been inside the Clifton's house?" I say it as nonchalantly as I can, but I still feel a quiver of nervous energy as I do.

He looks at me with that same rotten-smell expression on his face as before. "No. Why would I have?"

I shrug and turn away. "Did you know their daughter was dead?"

"Ah, what a shame. No. I didn't."

I'm no expert lie detector - especially after believing *He who will no longer be named* would be my forever person – but I believe Pete when he says this.

"I also found a large sum of money in the house," I say. "Which I thought was a bit strange." I don't take my eyes off him as I say this, and I notice his eyelid flickers. It could just be curiosity. I know what that feels like.

"How much are we talking?"

"Nearly two thousand pounds. But I thought it was odd how it was rolled up all tight with an elastic band around it. Like you see in the movies. Peggy said it was hers when I asked her about it - and fair enough, it was in her house so why wouldn't it be - but... I don't know..." I shake my head and laugh. "Shit. Ignore me I've had a tough week. I'm just being a drama queen."

Pete twists his mouth to one side as if thinking about what I've said. "Maybe," he says.

We drive on in silence for the next few minutes which gives me ample time to chastise myself for discussing the money with him. All at once the atmosphere in the car feels strained and I peer out the window until I sense the car slowing down.

"Are we here already?" I ask turning around.

"No, not yet. But I need to get some petrol," he says. "Sorry, I forgot. We've still got plenty of time. Your course starts at nine-fifteen, yes?"

"Erm, yes. That's right." I think I told him that the other night. I'm not sure.

We pull into a petrol station forecourt and he brings the car to a stop between the back set of pumps and the shop.

"Do you want anything?" Pete asks, clicking off his seat-belt. I can see through the shop window that there's a coffee machine on the back wall. If we're going to spend a few minutes here it might be worth getting a coffee now, rather than in the canteen at Samstone Manor. The coffee here is probably a lot nicer too, if not more expensive. But, in for a penny, in for a pound.

I climb out of the car and tell Pete my plan. He nods in acknowledgement and asks me if I can get him a large Americano with milk. I am rinsing this credit card today but it's the least I can do after he bought me dinner and is now giving me a lift.

He IS a nice guy. He has to be.

I enter the petrol station shop and head down the first aisle towards the coffee machine. It has a touchscreen display and paper cups in three sizes which protrude out of the fibreglass casing down one side. I remove two large cups - or rather, 'mega grande' cups to give them their branded names. The options are now 'grande', 'super grande' and 'mega grande'. Because who wants a small, right? I stuff the first one under the spout and make my selection on the screen. As the first drink is being made I turn around to take in the space. It's a standard petrol station with aisles full of brightly coloured magazines, overpriced snacks and a section containing oil, de-icer spray and other motor vehicle needs.

As I'm looking around Pete enters the shop and waves at me on his way to the counter. I wave back and hold up two fingers to tell him I'll be ready in that many minutes. He grins and holds up a credit card whilst pointing at the coffee machine - do I want him to pay for the drinks? I think about it for a moment but shake my head. I'll get them. I'm a grown woman. I don't need charity.

This is the first day of my new life.

This is me taking back control.

I turn to the coffee machine as the first drink is finished off with a burst of hot steam. I remove it from its metal cradle and shove in the next cup, before making the new selection. This time I watch the drink being made, engrossed as thin jets of coffee and milk spiral around each other as they fill the cup. Over my shoulder, I hear Pete calling over to me, but I can't tell what he's saying. I turn in time to see him leaving the shop and the door swinging shut behind him.

I grab the second coffee and carry both cups to the old man behind the counter. He doesn't look at me as he rings the coffees through the till, and I don't look at the price on the card reader machine as I swipe my credit card against it. It's fine. Give me a couple of months and I'll have paid my debts. This is how grown-ups do it. This is how people with proper jobs and real lives behave. I also console myself with the fact that using the card will be good for my credit rating in the long run. Buying my own house seems an impossible feat right now but I've got to start thinking of the future. I've spent too long stuck in the past.

I go outside to the car, but Pete isn't in the driver's seat as I expect him to be. As I step back I catch sight of him over on the far side of the forecourt. He's on his phone, pacing up and down behind the air and water machine. The stiff expression on his face and the way he's hunched over make give the impression the call is of a serious nature. As I watch he becomes more animated, barking into the receiver while gesticulating sharply with his other hand. At one point he looks over at the car and points right at me as if I'm the subject of his anger. He seems too engrossed in the conversation to notice me standing here but his aggressive mannerisms trouble me. He could just be telling his boss he'll be late because he's giving me a lift. That would be the innocent explanation.

He finishes the call and shakes his head at the phone before stuffing it in his trouser pocket. Then, he looks up and meets my eye and his face softens. I raise the coffee cups and give him a meek smile as he walks over.

"Sorry about that," he says and sighs pointedly. "Work stuff."

"It looked a bit intense," I say.

"It was nothing. Just my boss breathing down my neck to finish the project I'm working on." He opens the driver's door and climbs in before leaning over and opening my door an inch. I get my foot behind the bottom lip and leave it open enough that I can climb in whilst holding both coffee cups. "Right, let's get you to your course," Pete says.

I place Pete's coffee in the cup holder in front of the hand-brake and sip mine through the hole in the plastic top. It's hot and strong and I feel myself perking up as I drink. We make small talk – about the nice weather for the time of year, about the coffee – but finish the last leg of our journey in relative silence. Pete now seems tetchy and preoccupied but I'm pleased he's given up with the questions. Less than five minutes later Pete brings the car to a stop outside the entrance to Samstone Manor.

"Here we are." He turns off the engine and jumps out before I can respond. I hook my bag over the crook of my arm and, with my coffee in the other hand, get out. Pete is lifting my suitcase off the back seat as I join him on the other side of the car. He places it down and pulls up the handle for me. "All set."

An awkward silence – even more awkward than in the car just now – descends on us. I feel it in my sternum and up the back of my neck. I grimace and grin and nod, hoping some words might fall out of my mouth.

"Have you got everything?" he asks.

"Mm-hmm. Yes. All good." I look over his shoulder. "Well,

it's been nice to meet you, Pete. Thank you so much for the lift. And for listening to me whine. I'd ignore most of what I said though. The truth is I've no idea what's going on in that house and it's not my place to speculate." I only half-believe this as I say it but it's the right thing to say. Whoever Pete is, whatever he is, he needs to know I'm not a kooky amateur sleuth or anyone who might cause him trouble.

He smiles. "No worries, Lauren. I've enjoyed talking with you." He looks at his feet. "I don't suppose I could get your number. I know it's a bit of a distance, but I would like to see you again and—"

"Aww. No. Sorry. I don't think it's a good idea." His head snaps up and his forehead crumples. "You're a great guy, Pete. But I've just come out of a heavy relationship. I don't want to get involved with anyone, in any way, right now..."

I trail off as he holds his hand up. "That's fine. I get it. It was a stupid idea." He rubs his chin. "Take care of yourself, Lauren."

"And you." I shove my suitcase back onto its wheels and head for the entrance to the manor. Before I disappear through the gate I turn back and see him watching me with his hands in his pockets.

I still can't work this guy out. Is he just in need of a friend, or is there more to his interest than that? Whatever the answer, he's out of my life. I won't see him again. I wave at him and he waves back. He might be a great guy. He might even have been good for me. But it's not the right time. Besides, you wave everyone off eventually. And even great guys turn into bastards given time.

THIRTY

W e're an hour and thirty minutes into the first module of the day when I realise I haven't been listening to a word the tutor has been saying. I sit up and roll my shoulders back, glancing around at my fellow attendees. Martha with the good hair is looking my way but when our eyes meet, she smirks and turns away.

Was I doing something weird just now?

Was I talking to myself?

I know I was up in my head lost in a whirlwind of thought. As I shift my attention back to the present moment, I don't even remember what it was I was thinking about. But screw Martha with the good hair. Screw these people. They branded me an oddball earlier this week and no matter what I do now that's how they're going to view me. I don't care. I'll never see these women again. I've been an oddball my life and I don't need their approval.

Up at the front of the room, the tutor, a friendly lady with bright red hair, is explaining the assignment for this module. The subject is *Resourcing Talent* and we have to write three mock letters to candidates following a recent recruitment drive. One letter for the successful employee; one letter to a back-up candidate whose CV we want to keep on file; and one letter to send to all the unsuccessful people who didn't get the job. As Red explains this I can't help feeling it's all a bit too close to home. I'm probably going to fail this course and see a lot of this last sort of letter soon enough.

Buggering hell.

I'm such an idiot.

Why did I let myself get so caught up in the goings on at 47 Cranbourne Street? I should have been concentrating all my energy and determination into passing this course, yet I've only done the bare minimum needed and most likely will be returning to GP Telecom with my tail between my legs.

It's not like anyone has gained anything from all my focused worrying about Peggy and the possibility someone is taking advantage of her. As I sit here today surrounded by all these other people, I'm more certain than ever I've been viewing the events of this week through a paranoid, anxious state of mind. Peggy is just an old woman with a hazy memory and a longing for the world to be different. It's nice to believe if you *really* want your situation to change, that you can make it so - but you can't bring dead daughters back to life or mend fatally broken relationships and to think so is destructive in the long term. I'm reminded of something else Nana Mary used to say.

Hoping life will be different gets you nowhere and all prayer is just asking God to turn the blue sky green.

Nana Mary was a stoic woman. But kind with it. I smile at the memory of her as Red walks around the room and hands out printed documents relating to the module. Nana Mary died five years ago. I didn't go to her funeral because I was on holiday with Graham. He was dismissive that I'd even want to go pay my respects. She belonged to a world I was no longer a part of, he said. He didn't think I should equate myself with the person I was back then. He might have been right. He might have also been a selfish prick, who didn't want to cut his holiday short or consider his girlfriend was a care home kid.

I accept the handouts from the tutor and get to work on my letters, using the examples from the lecture to help me. It's easier than I imagined and as I complete the letter for the successful candidate, I'm rejuvenated by a fresh wave of confidence. If I do fail this course, it will be a total disaster, but I've already uploaded some of the assignments to the online training portal, and I doubt they'd allow me to continue each day if I was bombing out. Even so, I'm past caring. All I want is for this day to be over. As soon as I arrive at The Gilded Griffin I'm going to order room service and then have a long soak in a hot bubble bath. I might splash out on a nice bottle of wine. Why the hell not? I deserve some of the finer things in life after the week I've had. Then, tomorrow I'll complete this course and get the train back to Manchester. Ready to start my new life.

It's time to focus on Lauren Williams for a while. It's time to stop pining over losers who don't deserve me and rediscover my old tenacity and strength of mind. I used to be strong and independent. I used to trust myself. I used to be happy and…

Shit! No way!

Please, no!

Whilst considering this new resolve my hand has instinctively risen to the pendant on my mum's necklace. But I'm not wearing it! Sucking in a sharp breath I pat myself down, desperately hoping the clasp has come undone while I've been sitting here. But I already know where it is. In fact, I can picture exactly where is – lying on the bedside table in Peggy's spare room. In my hurry to book the hotel and get to the bus stop on time, I forgot to put it on this morning. This realisation is accompanied by a terrible sinking feeling.

I have to go back and get it.

I have to return to that damn house.

THIRTY-ONE

I spend the rest of the day talking myself into leaving the necklace behind. I tell myself I don't need it or even suit it, that this is a fresh start for me, that material possessions aren't important. At one point I even try to convince myself it's only brought me bad luck over the years. But as the afternoon session comes to a close, I know it's pointless. I need that necklace.

I have to return to Peggy's house.

On the bus back to Market Allerton I prep myself for my return. I'll knock on the door, inform Peggy what's happened and go straight upstairs to retrieve it. I'll tell her I'm in a hurry and be in and out of there as quickly as I can. I don't need to get into any conversations with her. I don't need to know what's going on with her or Rob. I'm there for the necklace. That is all. Work has paid for my stay in advance, so it's not like I owe them anything. Peggy is lovely and I have felt close to her this last week but I'm not her daughter. I'm nothing to do with her or Ron.

Once off the bus, I take my time walking to the house,

trying to psyche myself up as I go. When I get there, I knock on the door and step back to wait.

How ridiculous is it that I never got given a blasted key?

I don't understand how Peggy and Ron can keep advertising their house on VayCay Rooms whilst giving such terrible service. But then, I'm hardly going to sign onto the site and give them a bad review, am I? I couldn't do that to Peggy. Perhaps that's how it goes every time someone stays here. It's a terrible stay but you can't help liking the host. Then I remember that the house wasn't on the site when I looked and ponder whether past guests have complained and that's why the listing has been taken down. It makes sense. It's not fair to guests and it's not fair to Peggy and Ron. Plus, if they can afford to leave bundles of money lying around, they don't need the extra income.

I knock on the door again, louder and more urgent this time, before stepping to one side so I can look through the front room window. I can't see any movement, but they do spend most of their time in the kitchen. Leaning closer to the door I put my ear against the wood to listen. I can't hear anything but for some reason, I get the sense the house is occupied. Why wouldn't it be? Ron has his foot in a cast and isn't very mobile at the best of times. I knock again and this time I hear voices coming from the other side and the sound of chair legs scraping across the floor.

I straighten my back and put on a happy face as I hear shuffling behind the door and then the sound of a key in a lock. I swallow, going over the script in my head as I wait.

I can't stay.

I'm just here to collect my necklace.

I have to get my train.

The door opens a few inches and Peggy looks out through

the crack. She squints at me for a second and then her eyes sparkle in recognition.

"Oh? It's you, ducky," she says, but doesn't make any move to open the door wider.

"Hi, Peggy," I say. "Sorry to disturb you but I left something in my room. Do you mind if I run up and get it? I can't stay. I have to get my train."

Her face drops and she continues to clutch the edge of the door. "One second, dear," she says. "I'll be right back."

I baulk as she shuts the door in my face. This was not what I expected to happen. With the recovery mission I've been mentally rehearsing all the way here from Samstone Manor already in tatters, I wait on the doorstep for Peggy to return. After a long minute, I worry she's forgotten about me and am about to knock again when the door opens. This time Peggy looks happier to see me and her whole manner is more relaxed.

"Sorry about that," she says, stepping back to allow me to enter. "I had to…do something…all sorted now!"

I lift my suitcase over the stoop and step into the house after it. The slightly sweet, musky smell I've gotten used to over the past few days greets me as I close the door behind me. Peggy remains standing in the hallway, fiddling with her hands. She looks lost.

"Is everything okay?" I ask.

She lets her hands drop and looks up at me with a beaming smile. "Of course it is," she says, nodding as if trying to convince us both. "Come in. Come through to the kitchen. You're just in time. I've put the kettle on."

"Ah, no, Peggy. As I say, I've just come back for the necklace I left here. But I need to leave straight away. I've got a train to catch. Do you mind if I go up?" I step around her, about to head up the stairs when she holds her hand up.

"But you're here now. And so is Charlotte."

What?

I've got one foot on the first step, but I freeze. "Sorry?" I say. "Charlotte is here? Now?"

Peggy smiles. "That's right, dear. Why don't you come through and meet her? I think you'll get on like house on fire."

THIRTY-TWO

With my breath caught in my throat and my heart trying to beat its way out of my chest, I follow Peggy down the hallway to the kitchen. Ron is sitting in his usual place at the table and next to him, with her back to me, sits a young woman. She has blonde hair a similar shade to mine but cut into a shaggy bob and, as I enter the room, she shifts around in her seat and gives me a nod.

"All right, there. I'm Charlotte," she says. Her voice is deep, with the suggestion of a Liverpudlian accent.

"He-Hey," I stammer. "I'm Lauren. Pleased to meet you."

We stare at each other, and it feels as if time has stopped. She looks to be about my age or older – maybe even thirty-four, Charlotte's age if she was still alive. But I know she isn't alive. I've seen the coroner's documents and her death certificate. This woman, whoever she is, looks a little like Charlotte from the photos I've seen of her, but not so much you'd mistake the two of them. Even if you were hazy and forgetful.

So, what the hell is going on here?

"It's good to be back, isn't it love?" Ron pipes up, reaching out and grabbing the woman's arm. He gives it a gentle squeeze and I notice a flash of cruelty behind her eyes.

"It's great to be back," she says, not moving her eyes from mine as she shakes Ron's hand away. "I hear you've been staying here, Lauren. Is that right? In the spare room?"

I glance at Peggy who is staring down at her hands again. She picks at the skin around her thumbnail with the nail of her index finger.

"I've been doing a course over at Samstone Manor," I reply. "My employer booked this place for me."

"I see. Have you enjoyed yourself?" She flashes her eyes at me.

"Yeah. It's been...good. I didn't know if you'd be back while I was here. Peggy said you would, but..."

"I come back when I can. When I'm needed."

"Oh?"

The subtext in the air is almost oppressive as we both play nice in front of Peggy. I assume this woman knows that I know she isn't the Cliftons' daughter. But what she's doing here is another matter.

Who is she? What does she want?

"Peggy – *Mum* – tells me you'd vacated the room," the woman says. "I'm surprised to see you back here."

"Yeah. I wasn't planning on returning but I left something in the room. I came back to get it."

She winks. "Got ya!"

The room falls silent. Every cell in my body is desperate to get the necklace and get the hell out of here but I remain where I am. After what seems like forever Peggy tuts loudly and the tension subsides.

"What am I playing at?" she says. "I'll put the kettle on and make us all a nice cup of tea."

"Not for me..." I start but she's already picked up the kettle and is walking over to the sink. I watch as she busies herself clinking cups around before turning my attention back to the woman at the table.

"Is there a problem?" she asks, glaring at me.

"You tell me." I sense my system filling with adrenaline, and I take a deep breath to steady myself. "What's going on?"

"What do you mean? I've come back to see my mum and dad. To make sure everything is going well here." She sniffs. "Do *you* think something's wrong?"

"No. I never said that." I hold her gaze, trying to work out her angle. Clearly, anyone who is impersonating an elderly couple's dead daughter is bad news, but how bad is unclear. "And you're Charlotte - Charlotte Clifton – Peggy and Ron's daughter?"

She tilts her head to one side and puts on a big cheesy smile. "That's me."

I want to slap her. I look at Ron, who is staring into space with his mouth hanging open, lost to the world.

"Hmm," I reply. "That's strange."

"Is it?" She scrapes her chair back and stands. She's an inch taller than me but sinewy. As she turns to face me her expression is intense and stern. "No danger here, is there?" she whispers, lowering her chin. "They think I'm their long-lost daughter and I go along with it. For them. I visit, I have a cup of tea and a sandwich, they like looking after me. It makes them happy. So...leave it." She says this last part through gritted teeth as she steps towards me.

She's so close now I can smell her. Her scent is a mixture of body odour and cheap perfume.

"And what's in it for you?" I ask, my eyes flitting from hers to Peggy and back again. The old woman is still fussing over the tea with her back to us and can't hear our conversation.

"I told you," she snarls. "I get a cup of tea, a sandwich - or a cake if I'm lucky - and we have a nice chat. They're nice people. Look at them both. Salt of the Earth." She stares deep into my eyes. I'm aware she's trying to intimidate me, but I hold my ground and keep my head up. This, despite the intense panic fluttering in my belly.

Whatever this woman says, I doubt she's here because of some altruistic gesture of goodwill. I'm the last person to judge anyone based on how they look or sound, but I've been around enough dodgy people in my life to know one when I see one. All I can think is that she's taking advantage of Peggy and Ron somehow - and it's not for cake. Otherwise, why not visit as herself rather than pretending to be Charlotte? Why put this poor old couple through this sick pantomime?

Also, I don't like the way she's looking at me. It's as if she's trying to work me out as much as I am her. The false affability she displayed on my arrival has now gone and in its place, I detect an air of menace. She's trying to work out if I'm a threat to her.

I make the decision there and then. As soon as I'm safely in my room at The Gilded Griffin I'll call the police and report everything I've seen here today. Until now I was unsure how to frame my suspicions, but if I explain to them that this person is coming into the Clifton's house under false pretences, they'll have to take me seriously.

Decision made; I feel a little more confident as I step out from imposter Charlotte's glare.

"No tea for me, thanks, Peggy," I tell her. "I really do need to leave. I'm going to go get my necklace and get off if you don't mind." I'm backing away into the hallway when she turns around with a crestfallen look on her face.

"You've no time for a cup of tea?"

I stop in the doorway. "No. I'm sorry."

"Ah go on."

The woman who isn't Charlotte pushes past me. "You should stay a while," she says, speaking through gritted teeth. "Have a cup of tea with us all. It'll be nice. I just need to make a quick phone call. I'll be back in a minute."

A shiver takes me over as I watch her walk down the hallway and go into the front room. I give it a few seconds then direct my attention back to Peggy.

"I really do have to leave," I whisper. "I'm so sorry. But I'm going to help you. I promise."

She smiles at this but it's not her usual smile. Now there's something else behind the façade. It could be reluctance; it could be fear; it could even be gratitude. Or I could be imagining all of it.

Leaving Peggy in the kitchen I creep down the hallway past the front room. As I get to the doorway I see the woman standing in front of the television set, facing the window. She has an old-fashioned, flip-style phone clamped to the side of her head and with her back to the door she doesn't see me. She's speaking softly and every so often she nods profusely in response to whatever the person on the other end is saying. I get the impression she's receiving some sort of instruction. I continue on my path but as I reach the bottom of the stairs her voice grows in volume.

"You're the boss," I hear her say. "If you say it needs to happen, then consider it done."

I don't like the sound of that. I race up the stairs taking them two and a time and stride across the landing and into the spare room. The necklace is exactly where I pictured it on the bedside table. I scoop it up and stuff it into my pocket. I could put it on but that would take time and I have to get out of this house before that sinister woman finishes her call.

I move across the landing without taking a breath and lean into the banister on my way down the stairs to allow it to take some of my weight. I'm out of here. It's done. I can almost feel the relief flooding through me but as I reach the bottom few steps my heart turns to stone and drops into my stomach. Peggy and the woman are standing in the hallway and as I take the last few steps the woman moves in front of the door.

"Oh, hi again," I say, but my voice sounds shaky as hell. "I have to leave for my train now. Nice to see you both."

The woman cricks her neck from side to side. She moves behind my suitcase and grabs the upright handle. "Actually, I've got a better idea."

"Oh?" I step down onto the ground floor. "And what's that?"

"I was just saying to Mum, here. I've got my car outside and I'm going near the train station. Why don't I give you a lift?"

"Oh. Right. Yeah."

I look from the woman to Peggy as a fresh surge of adrenaline floods my system. It makes me shudder, but I tense the muscles in my upper body so it's not apparent. Or so I hope. Because I can't let this person know I'm scared. Or suspicious. Or that I feel anything towards her other than neutral. Right now, she's unsure what I know - about the money, about what she's doing here, about the abuse – and I want it to stay that way.

Peggy smiles at me and nods. "It's okay, dear."

Okay for her? Or for me?

I stare into the old woman's eyes, trying to work out just how much she understands about what's going on here. Is she a willing participant in this farce? Is she so broken by grief she'll accept anyone with a forced smile, happy to play the role of her daughter?

"Do you know what? It's fine." I return my attention to the imposter Charlotte who is still clutching the handle of my suitcase. "My train isn't for a few hours. And I think I'd like the walk. It's a pleasant evening."

"Don't be silly. The station is over an hour away on foot," she says, punctuating each sentence with an incredulous giggle. "Plus, it's dark out. And it's getting cold. You don't want to be walking the streets at this time of night."

"I don't mind."

"I insist." She smiles as I reach for the handle of my case but won't let go. "Honestly, Lauren. I want to give you a lift."

"Charlotte can take you to the station," Peggy adds.

"I don't need her to," I reply, the two of us still clutching onto the suitcase handle. "I can walk. I'd prefer it that way."

The woman steps around the side of the case towards me. I tense, half-expecting her to hit me but she leans in so her face is next to mine.

"Listen, Lauren. It's simple," she hisses in my ear. "You want to get away from here. I'd like that too. So let me take you. That way, we're both happy. Do you get me? Everything is taken care of." She's standing so close I can feel her hot breath on my cheek. As she leans back, she doesn't blink or take her eyes off mine.

She has a point, I suppose. It's in her best interests to have me as far away as possible. And that's what I'd like also. But to get into a car with her. Can I? Should I?

Before I have a chance to answer these questions the

woman yanks the suitcase out of my grip and reaches out for the door handle.

Oh look, it's open for once. What are the chances?

"Come on, Lauren," she says with a smile. "I'll put your suitcase in the car. You say goodbye to Mum and follow me out." With that, she swings open the door, picks up my case and leaves.

I turn back to Peggy who is still smiling sweetly despite her crooked fingers being intertwined in a knot of disquiet. But I get it. My stomach is doing the same thing.

"I'll be fine," I tell her. "And so will you and Ron. I'm going to make sure of it."

She nods. "It was nice to have you here, dear. You take care."

"I will."

A voice from outside calling my name stops any further chat. I pull in a deep breath. Whether I can, or should, go with this woman was answered just now when passiveness or fear – or the fact I didn't want to cause a scene in front of Peggy - had me let go of my suitcase. The suitcase that is now in the boot of her car with my passport and laptop inside it. I had to jump through so many hoops to get that passport and I still have assignments saved on the laptop that I need to upload to the training portal so I can complete my course.

My future is inside that case.

I can't let her drive away with it.

I give Peggy a final stoic grin and then leave the house.

THIRTY-THREE

I step outside to see the woman a few metres away on this side of the street. She holds her hand up to get my attention. Like I needed her to do that. Like my attention isn't already bristling on high alert. She's standing next to an old silver Ford Escort with '98 plates and enough rust on the bodywork you could make the joke it was this alone holding it together.

As I walk up to her, I almost ask if she thinks the car will get us to the station, but the words die on my tongue as I see the look in her eyes. The friendly façade she exhibited in Peggy's kitchen has gone and the streetlight overhead casts hollow shadows on her face. I'd call her skinny, rather than slim, but that doesn't mean she'd be a pushover. I've met people with the same wiry frame over the years who could cut me down with a few choice movements. She's wearing tight dark blue jeans and purple ankle boots. On her top half, she wears a scruffy green army surplus jacket. I stop next to the car. My suitcase stands on the road in front of her. She hasn't put it in the car yet. I've still time to get away.

"Hey, Lauren. Don't look so worried," she says as if reading my thoughts. "The station is only fifteen minutes away. I know my old car isn't much to look at but it runs well enough."

She places a hand on the roof and leans down to unlock the boot with a key.

"I'm not actually going to the station," I blurt out. "I told Peggy that because I didn't want to upset her. The truth is, I've booked myself into a hotel. I fancied something...different for my last night."

The woman lifts open the boot hatch and turns to me. A wide smirk spreads across her face. "I don't blame you," she says. "But that's cool. Which hotel?"

I stare at her, wondering if I should lie. But what would be the point?

"The Gilded Griffin," I say.

She purses her lips. "I know it. I can drop you there no problem." Before I can reply she hauls my suitcase up into the back of her car and slams the boot door shut.

Well, that's that then. She has all my worldly possessions locked in her car. And I've just let it happen like some pathetic coward.

What the hell is going on?

I can't imagine the old Lauren being cowed so easily, but it's hard to know how you'll react in a situation until you're presented with it. But what is this situation? I know I can't trust this woman. But the question I need to answer is, does she mean me harm? Does she consider me a threat? I do want to get away from 47 Cranbourne Street just as much as she wants to get rid of me. So, is that all that's happening here? Is she giving me a lift so she knows I'm out of the way?

"You don't have to do this," I try, holding my hands up. "I can get a taxi or something…"

She pushes past me and walks around to the driver's door. "It's not a problem. I've told you that," she says. "In fact, The Gilded Griffin is closer to where I'm going than the train station. It works out well." She smiles proudly as if she's got an answer for everything. I suppose she has. I look back and see Peggy standing in the doorway of her house. She waves and I wave back.

Should I say something? Should I tell her where I'm really going? If I say it loud enough other people on the street might hear me. I glance around, trying to locate Pete's house. In all the excitement I can't remember what number he said it was. I look up at one of the top windows in the house two doors down and see someone looking down at us. As soon as our eyes meet, they step back out of sight but not before I notice they have black shoulder-length hair. That's weird. I'm sure that's Pete's house.

"Lauren! Say goodbye and get in the car!" I spin around to see the woman glaring at me. She nods at Peggy over my shoulder. "You wouldn't want to upset her, would you? You wouldn't want to do anything that might hurt her?"

I raise my chin. "No."

"Good. Me neither. Get in the car."

There's a flicker of malice in her eyes that I recognise all too well. She wants me to know she's not someone to be messed with. But neither am I. And I certainly don't want this bitch to think she's getting to me.

Planting a confident smile on my face I wander around the side of the car. I feel numb but also like I'm vibrating with energy. I open the door and climb in, having to trample down the pile of McDonald's wrappers that litter the footwell. The rest of the car is just as messy, with sweets wrappers and empty drink cans covering the back seat and a layer of grime on the dashboard. A sickly odour of fake strawberry fights for dominance over the stale air. The car rocks as the woman climbs into the driver's seat beside me and slams her door shut.

"Right, then. Let's go."

She starts the engine and shoves the stick in first. I reach around and pull the seat belt over me and, as we pull away from the kerb, I see Peggy waving at us in the rear-view mirror. She remains there until we get to the end of the street and then disappears from sight as we take a left towards the main road.

I grab the door handle, wondering if I could survive throwing myself out of a speeding car if the need arose. But as we pull onto the high street and the car picks up speed, I decide I couldn't.

"Everything okay?" the woman asks.

I shoot her a look. "I don't know. You tell me."

"You seem very stressed."

I scoff. I can't help myself. "I wonder why?" I shift in my seat, so my back is against the door. A ripple of nervous energy prickles the skin on my forearms and down the back of my neck. "Are you going to tell me your real name?" I ask.

The woman laughs as if I'm being ridiculous. "You've got the wrong idea about me, Lauren. Honestly. I'm not who you think I am."

"You're not who Peggy thinks you are. You're not Charlotte. You're not her daughter."

"No. I'm not. Of course I'm not. We both know that."

"Good. So, who are you?"

I try to stay calm. But the bubble of anxiety I've carried in my diaphragm since seeing this woman sitting at Peggy's kitchen table stops me from taking a full breath. I feel as if I'm on the edge of a panic attack. I focus my energy on staying on the right side of it as the woman sighs and readies herself to respond.

"My real name is Karen," she says. "But I did know Charlotte Clifton."

"Really?"

"Yeah. She was a good kid. Troubled, but funny." She smiles to herself as if remembering. "I don't think she got on with her mum and dad towards the end. She said they were old-fashioned. Apparently, they wouldn't let her go out, or have boyfriends, or do anything teenagers do. They were kind enough, just strict. I think Charlotte and them clashed quite a bit. Then when she was old enough, she ran away to Liverpool. That's where I met her."

"You got her into drugs?"

She makes a dramatic *pfft* noise, spraying spittle over the windscreen. "She didn't need any encouragement believe me. She was already well into the smack when I met her. I tried to help her. But I couldn't."

I don't take my eyes off Karen as she talks. I'm trying to work out if I can believe her. She seems genuine enough.

"Why are you pretending to be her?"

"Oh behave," she snaps, sounding more Liverpudlian than ever. "I'm not *pretending*. Not really. When Charlie died, I came down here to visit her mum and dad. They're nice people. But you must have picked up on the fact they're both pretty forgetful."

"Yes. I have. They're old and vulnerable. They need proper help and support."

"I know that. But they also want to stay in that house. The

place they've called home for the last fifty-plus years. So, I help them do that. I care for them. I look out for them. I help them with money and paying their bills and such like."

"You care for them?"

"Yes. I do."

She looks right at me. Her eyes are intense, and her mouth is twisted into a cruel sneer. She doesn't look very caring.

"It was Ron who started calling me Charlotte," she continues. "At first it was just now and again, a slip of the tongue but the more confused he grew the more it happened. After a while, I stopped correcting him. I think Peggy just goes along with it. I think she likes to pretend. Poor old girl."

"I see."

I shift around in my seat and stare out the side window as I consider her words.

Have I got this all wrong?

Is she speaking the truth?

This explanation sounds plausible enough, yet there's something about Karen I don't like. My fingers snake around the door release handle whilst, at the same time, my other hand finds the seat belt clasp. Two clicks and I could be out of here. She's got my suitcase, but I can get the car registration number and ring the police as soon as I'm clear of her.

"Don't be daft, Lauren," Karen says, reading my mind once more. "You could seriously hurt yourself. Besides, that door is broken. It only opens from the outside."

"No. I wasn't…" I splutter, shunting around to face her again. "I mean. I'm fine."

She remains watching the road and doesn't look my way, but she's smirking to herself. "You're too smart for your own good, aren't ya?"

I sit back in my seat, trying to ignore the uneasy feeling

rising in my guts. But I can't dismiss it. I shouldn't. My instincts *are* good. I should have believed in myself from the start.

As if to further highlight this and slam another nail in my coffin I see a sign for The Gilded Griffin up ahead, on my side of the road. At the same time as Karen puts her foot down on the accelerator and I turn and watch as we speed past the entrance.

I point out the window. "That was—"

"Yes! I know it was." We speed on down the road.

"Hey! Let me out!" I cry, yanking the slack and unresponsive door release handle. "That was my hotel. You need to turn around and go back."

Karen laughs. "I can't do that. Sorry."

"You don't have to worry about me," I tell her. "I'm a nobody. I swear to you. Whatever is going on I don't care. I don't care who you are or what you're doing. I just want to go home. Please stop the car." Regardless of the broken handle, it doesn't stop me from pulling on it, desperate to open the door. My heart feels as if it's about to burst.

Karen eyes me and shakes her head. "You know I did want to let you go,' she says and her voice is so soft and her tone so matter of fact it jolts me out of my panic. I swallow, which is difficult with a knot of emotion stuck in my throat.

"Then let me go," I say.

She cricks her head to one side and makes a tutting noise. "We were going to. That was the plan. We knew things had messed up with the house but that was our fault and when I came to check on things and found you gone, we were happy to leave it at that. At first..." She looks at me and raises an eyebrow. "But then Peggy handed me this." She slides her hand into her jacket pocket and pulls out the roll of money I found in the spare room. Holding it up to me she shakes her head and makes another tutting noise. "You've been snooping around. Looking into things you shouldn't have been. What did you think when you found this?"

"I didn't think anything. Peggy said it was hers and I accepted that. I assumed it was their savings or something."

"Is that right? Rolled up like this? You're Little Miss Innocent, is that it?" She smirks and returns the money to her pocket. "You need to work on your acting skills, Lauren. They're terrible."

"I won't say anything," I say. "Please I—"

Karen lets out a sigh that sounds more like a roar and I shut up. She grabs the steering wheel with both hands and twists them around as if wringing a bird's neck.

"Listen, yeah, I'm sorry," she says. "But it's been decided. You know too much. You're a problem. Plus, you've seen my face now. We can't have that I'm afraid."

The muscles across my chest tighten as fight-or-flight hormones flood my system. "What's been decided?" I ask. "Where are you taking me?"

She doesn't answer.

"Where are we going?" I try.

"You'll see. It's not long now until we get there."

I gulp down a shiver of fear. "Are you going to kill me?"

She sniffs and cricks her neck to one side again but doesn't reply. And I can't help but think that means, yes.

She's going to kill me.

When this car stops, I'm going to die.

THIRTY-FOUR

I'm not sure how long we've been driving. Time seems to have slowed down to a stop. I can't think straight or even form a sentence. I tell myself to take some deep breaths to try to slow my heart rate but all I can manage are stuttering staccato gasps.

Come on, Lauren.

Fight it. Keep it together.

Things look desperate right now but it's not over yet. I manage to get behind my breathing but as I inhale deeply it brings with it a fresh wave of emotion. I bite the side of my fist as a yelp of panic escapes me.

Karen sneers. "Don't be so pathetic."

"I'm not being pathetic!" I yell back. "I've been through a lot, all right. A hell of a lot. You don't know. You don't know me."

She snickers to herself. "*You don't know me,*" she repeats in a scornful London accent. Her face drops and she throws me a nasty look, lowering her voice in the process. "No. *You* don't know *me*, Lauren. Or my boss. You've no idea who you're dealing with."

I don't understand why she's still trying to intimidate me. She's already alluded to the fact I'm about to die. Why would I care who she is other than my prospective killer?

But her being this way only riles me rather than scares me. It makes me more determined than ever that I won't go down without a fight. I get the impression Karen thinks I'm some posh pathetic princess type. A poor defenceless girl who was in the wrong place at the wrong time. Well, I certainly was in the wrong place, but I'm no princess. I've fought off bigger and nastier people than Karen before.

I'm aware this is the only ace I've got up my sleeve – if you can even call it that – so I'll play up to the meek princess role for now. Let the scrawny bitch underestimate me.

And…oh, shit!

A surge of anticipation courses through my veins as I realise I still have my phone with me. It's tucked away in my trouser pocket, right by the door. If I can extract it without Karen noticing, I can call the police. Keeping my eyes on the road and my head still, I move my arm back and ease my hand into my pocket. It's not easy, but I manage to get my fingers on the cold plastic phone casing, carefully inching it out with minimal motion. If I call emergency services and don't speak, my hope is the operator will pick up on the fact something is wrong. They'll be able to trace the call and find out my location.

I'm on the verge of liberating my phone when the car violently jolts over a speed bump. The impact wrenches the device from my grasp, sending it clattering into the crevice between the seat and the door. My heart leaps into my throat as I look up.

Karen is glaring at me "That was bloody stupid!"

I remain silent, my fingers desperately probing the narrow gap, seeking my lost lifeline. I suck in a sharp breath as my index finger brushes against it but the phone is beyond reach. It's gone.

Damn it!

"I told you to behave." Karen snarls.

"You can't blame me for trying." I mumble, my heart plummeting. I scan the car for alternative escape options, but there are none.

Karen chuckles. "You've got some balls; I'll give you that."

I slump back into my seat, gazing at my hazy reflection in the window as we race past a sprawling industrial park and enter a network of streets with rows of terraced houses on either side. We drive past a lone figure walking a dog and as we turn onto the next street Karen puts her foot down on the accelerator.

I have another day.

Subtly repositioning myself on my seat, I extend my legs to reach the footwell's depths. I have one shot at this. If I can wrestle control of the wheel from Karen, I might be able to drive us into a wall and make a break for it. It's risky as hell but I'm out of alternatives. I brace myself, steeling my resolve and telling myself I'll go for it the second Karen rounds the next corner.

As we make the turn I'm poised to act. But my heart clenches at the sight of a group of children loitering by the roadside.

No.

Damn it.

I can't do it. I can't risk the car ploughing into those kids. I force my tense muscles to relax and exhale a defeated sigh. When I glance up, I find Karen smirking at me.

"Don't even think about it," she says, leaning over and unfastening my seatbelt. As it retracts into its compartment, she adds, "There are no airbags in this old heap. If you try and make us crash, you'll be the one going through the windscreen."

"I-I wasn't…" I stammer.

"No. Of course you weren't." She sneers. "Good as gold you, aren't ya?"

I cross my arms, feeling even more vulnerable without the seatbelt's embrace. We drive on in tense silence for several more minutes. I consider making a move for the wheel anyway, but my body refuses to comply. Besides, it's suicidal.

"Don't take it personally," Karen says as we leave the terraced streets behind and the road stretches out before us. "It's just business."

I stare out the window and try to ignore her, but then I remember something.

"What did you mean before?" I ask. "You said it was your fault that things in the house had got messed up."

Karen presses her lips together and sniffs. I get the impression she's deciding whether to answer.

"Some prick lower than me on the food chain made a mistake," she mutters, before indicating right and taking the car down a long road. What look to be derelict warehouses spread out in front of us on either side. "He listed the wrong address on the listing site. We've used Peggy's spare room before but only for those involved in the organisation. With them owning that place, we don't have to show it being used like some of our other properties."

I close one eye. I'm trying hard to keep up, but I don't

understand. "So, you didn't want people staying there or you did?"

"We own a lot of properties in the area. They're used for different things. In periods when we aren't using them, we rent them out, so it doesn't look suss. It should have been the property across the street that was advertised but this guy, Marek, entered the details for Peggy's place by mistake. It should have been an easy catch. But then you turned up at forty-seven. I bet those two old fools welcomed you in like they were expecting you, didn't they? Shit. They're so desperate for company, poor old bastards." She sniffs back again and I can hear the phlegm in her throat. It makes me nauseous. "We took the property off the site as soon as we realised what had happened, but you were already in there. You gave us a scare at first but after a lengthy discussion and once we'd got a look at you, we were happy for you to stay the week and then piss off. But you had to get nosey, didn't you? Snooping around. That's a shame, that is."

She slows the car and pulls it around a sharp bend which brings us out on the edge of a sprawling concrete wasteland. Over to my left, it looks as if the world has dropped away but as I peer through the window, I realise it's the edge of a jetty. We're next to water and most likely somewhere up near Liverpool, so I assume it to be the River Mersey. We drive alongside the river across the wasteland, heading towards a large building that looks like an old factory on the other side.

A dirty old van is parked in front of the building and Karen brings the car to a stop twenty feet away from it. I sit up, my hands balled up into fists. She switches off the engine and looks me up and down. The tendons in my hands are so tight they burn.

"I thought I told you to behave," Karen says, her eyes

widening. "There are two ways this can go now, Lauren. I'll be honest with you; you're not going to like either option but one is definitely a lot worse. Do you get me?"

I bite down hard on the back of my lip to stop it from wobbling. "Yes." My voice sounds muted like it's coming from another place and time. Karen regards me for what seems like forever before shaking her head and opening the car door. She climbs out and rolls her shoulders back before leaning down to address me.

"Wait here," she says, shutting the door and locking it.

I sit for a second but as soon as she walks over to the van I unbuckle my seat belt and shuffle onto the driving seat. She might have locked the door from the outside, but I can easily pop the lock knob up and...

Shit!

No!

I run my fingers down the material under the window. There is no knob. Just a hole where it should be. Stupid old cars. I try the door release handle but it's no use. The door is locked. I'm locked in here. I cast my attention over the dashboard, searching desperately for a magic button that will unlock the doors and set me free. But it's all analogue and manual controls.

Bloody, stupid old cars.

I scramble back onto the passenger seat, still looking around the car but now for something I could use as a weapon. A car jack, a wrench, anything. In the footwell of the back seat, I find an old plastic cigarette lighter and an empty beer bottle. I reach down for them and sit back in my seat as the van's headlights switch on. They shine right in my face, dazzling me. I recoil, holding my hand up in front of my eyes to protect them from the glare. The lights dip and as I blink to rid myself of the red spiders clouding my vision, I see Karen standing next to the van and a large man standing beside her. He has a thick black beard and is wearing a dark navy beanie hat. He's one of the men I saw in the backyard earlier this week, I'm certain of it.

But of course he is. These creeps own the whole street. The whole town perhaps. I gasp. That means Pete must be a part of this, too.

You idiot.

Why didn't I trust myself back when I first suspected something was wrong? I should have called work straight away and told them I didn't feel safe in the accommodation they'd provided. They'd have understood. They'd have had to take it seriously, at least. But no. I allowed my insecurities to get the better of me. I ignored my better judgement. And now I'm going to die here, in this deserted car park. Alone and scared.

But I suppose that's fitting.

Alone and scared is how I've felt for most of my life.

THIRTY-FIVE

I watch through the car window, my chest rising and falling with each breath, as Karen and the man talk over by the van. I can't tell what they're saying but I imagine they're discussing what they're going to do with me. How they're going to do...*it*. I think back to earlier, in Peggy's house. At one point I think Karen was going to let me go but then she made that phone call and her whole demeanour changed. Whoever was on the other end of that line must be the one calling the shots, but I don't think it was the man in the beanie hat. He looks like muscle rather than brains. That means that Karen and he are merely foot soldiers. They don't make the decisions.

I've no idea if this realisation is helpful, but thinking about it keeps my mind from running away with itself. If I have any chance of walking away from this situation I have to stay focused.

Because it's true, being alone and scared has been my default setting for most of my life, but you can also add tenacity and anger to that setting. Especially as I got older.

Every counsellor and therapist that I've ever sat in front of has told me that I need to work on my anger - that it would stop me from becoming the person I can be. But I know differently. In some situations, it's helpful. Anger isn't a bad emotion. Not when it's justified. Not when it can give you the energy to survive.

Shit!

I sit up as Karen and the man start walking towards me.

This is it!

As they get nearer to the car, I tighten my grip on the neck of the beer bottle holding it down, below the level of the seat. Karen gets to the car first and opens the passenger door.

"Out," she barks, stepping back to give me space. "Now."

The man folds his arms and stares at me. Up close, he looks even bigger and scarier. His skin is tanned and weathered, and his eyes are so dark I can't see his pupils, even in the bright headlights of the van.

"Get out," he growls, in a heavy accent.

"Please, you've got to understand," I say. "I'm not a threat to you. I'm not some do-gooder. I hate the authorities just as much as you do. I was in care since I was a little kid The system has screwed me over all my life. I would never dream of grassing anyone to the police. Or to anyone." I'm speaking fast. In survival mode. I hold my free hand out to the two of them. "Spare me. Let me go. I won't tell anyone. I promise…"

"Save it, Lauren." Karen looks away with a sneer. "I've got your phone, remember."

"But I wasn't going to use it."

"You were trying to. Get out of the car!"

"Karen, please. I'm sorry. Let me go. You don't have to do this."

She lowers her head and sighs. "Yes. I do. We can't take any chances. There are too many police sniffing around at the moment. All weak links have to be taken out."

The man clears his throat. "Weak links."

I glance from him to Karen as I adjust my grip on the neck of the bottle. As soon as I step out of the car, they'll see me holding it and that'll be it. I need one of them to come closer.

"What will happen to Peggy and Ron?" I ask.

"They'll be fine. Like always," Karen snaps. "We'll keep on using their spare room for stash and, in return, I'll keep playing nice. You do know we pay them for their troubles, don't you? Plus, they're both practically housebound. How do you think they get their groceries?"

As she's talking, I'm scanning the area without making it obvious, looking for escape routes, things on the ground I might use as a weapon. Anything. I feel sick and desperate, and time is ticking away.

One last try.

"Listen, Karen. I know you're not a bad person. You care about the Cliftons, I can tell. Let me go. I'll get the train back to Manchester and I won't tell anyone what I've seen or what happened here. Not a soul."

Karen chews on her lip. Her face is twisted in frustration but is she faltering? I stare at her, willing her to look into my eyes. To see I'm telling the truth. For now, at least. I shake any other thoughts away. When she looks into my face, she has to see I mean what I say.

"Please, Karen. It doesn't have to be this way…"

She glances at the big man and my heart flips over. It looks as if she's softening, but before she can speak the moment is broken by the shrill ring of a mobile phone.

Karen turns away and pulls her phone out of her pocket. I lean out of the car to listen as she answers.

"Yes… We're here with Maz…. She says not… No. I'm not sure… Yes… Yes, I get it. Okay. Say no more." She hangs up and when she turns around she doesn't look at me. That's when I know it's over.

It's not fair.

I never had a chance.

This can't be how I die.

I think of Peggy and Ron, I think of Graham, then I think of Nana Mary and even my mum.

"Maz," Karen juts her chin at the big man. "He says to deal with her in the usual way. Do it quickly. Do it now."

THIRTY-SIX

I yelp as the big man – Maz - steps around the side of the car and grabs my arm. I struggle against him, but his grip is strong and his nails dig into the thin flesh under my arm.

"Hey, get off," I call out.

"Out!"

He yanks me up and out of the car. As he does, I swing the bottle at him. The glass neck jars against my palm as it connects with the side of his head, but the bottle remains intact. Maz looks shocked. Then confused. Then angry. He lets go of my arm and rounds on me, baring his teeth. I swing the bottle again, but he dodges out of the way and backhands me across the face, knocking me against the car.

"Stupid bitch."

"What the hell is going on?" Karen yells

As the pain spreads through my skull I fling the bottle at her. She ducks out of the way but in doing so loses her footing and stumbles over. As Maz turns to her I push past him, putting his hulking frame between Karen and I as I make a run for it.

"Get her."

A hand brushes my shoulder, but I shift my weight over to dodge the grab. With my head down I race across the barren industrial lot towards the warehouse. I'm free but I'm not sure what to do next. Where do I go? What do I do? It feels like I'm floating on air as the past, present and future all rush to meet me in an explosion of sensory overload. A voice in my head tells me, *Run!*

Keep running!

With my head down I race across the barren concrete towards the warehouse. I have no plan. All I know is I have to put as much distance between myself and those bastards as possible. Behind me, I hear them shouting at each other and then the sound of heavy footsteps echoing across the wasteland as they chase after me.

Gritting my teeth, I press on, running as fast as my legs will take me. As I get closer to the warehouse, I see a high metal fence running down the side of the lot which creates a passageway between it and the building about the width of a car. The passageway appears to lead around to the back of the warehouse but it's too dark to see what's down there. On the other side of the warehouse are the jetty and the river but it's too out in the open. I head for the passageway hoping the darkness might act as cover. As I head down the side of the building a sonic crack breaks the air and I almost run into the wall out of shock.

I look back and my worst fear is confirmed. Karen is holding a gun. She aims at me and the space lights up as a second gunshot echoes through my skull. This time I feel the bullet whizzing past me a few feet away.

That was close.

Too close.

I run down the side of the building and am immediately plunged into darkness. I slow my pace in case I run into something, swaying my arms out in front of me as I negotiate a path through the gloom. As my eyes grow accustomed, I see an old bricked-up doorway to my left and a row of large industrial waste bins standing against the side of the building further down. At the far end, it looks to open out onto a thin strip of concrete and in the light offered by a far-off streetlamp I can make out a grass incline leading up to a low wall and then a row of trees. Behind the trees is more high metal fencing.

I grind my teeth together. Maybe I could scale one of the trees and get over the fence but it's risky with Karen and Maz so close behind me. I decide against it. I have to outrun them. Or outwit them. Hopefully both.

I press on, taking wide strides and going up onto the balls of my feet so I make less noise. Once I get past the industrial waste bins I stop and drop to my knees, resting my back against the side of the building. I can hear footsteps at the far end of the passage. They're no longer running but moving steady and quietly. On the hunt.

"Lauren! Cooome oooouut!" Karen sings. "You're only delaying the inevitable, *ducky*."

Now my eyes have grown fully accustomed to the dim light I can see the area is littered with old wooden storage pallets and cardboard boxes. There's also what looks like a metal bar on the other side of the passage, next to the fence. Slowly, I lean around the side of the nearest waste bin, but I can't see anyone. Are they hiding? Lying in wait for me to make a mistake?

I rock forward on my feet. The metal bar could be a useful

weapon in other circumstances, but is it any use against a gun? Especially if, by trying to get it, Karen has a clear shot at me.

No. Too risky.

I remain in a crouching position and crab-walk down the side of the warehouse until I get to the far end. Once I'm around the corner out of sight I get to my feet and pause. It's hard to hear anything over my erratic breathing but when I hold my breath, I can hear footsteps and someone whispering. They're getting closer. Yet I get the impression they think I'm hiding behind the bins. I hear Karen say, "Down there."

I push off from the wall and run down the back of the building, moving up onto the grass incline so I make less noise. As I go, I keep one eye over to my right, searching for a gap in the fence or a particularly climbable tree that might transport me to freedom. But neither appears. At the next corner, I stop and turn back. Karen and Maz are nowhere in sight and a shiver of excitement rushes down my neck. If I can make it down to where the cars are parked without them catching me, I can escape down one of the many side streets we passed on the way here. As long as I put enough distance between me and them, I've got a fighting chance. Then all I need is a fast-food outlet or a pub. Somewhere that can provide sanctuary while I call the police.

It'll be over.

It'll all be over.

Buoyed by this realisation I turn the corner and sprint down the side of the building. Up close, the River Mersey smells salty and tidal. A family of large seagulls bob serenely on the water, watching me as I race past. A sharp stitch pierces my side and the muscles on my legs burn with exertion, but I don't stop. Another thirty seconds and I'll have reached the far side of the building, another minute I'll be over the other side of the wasteland and away. I can do this. I can do it. I can— No!

"Shit! Bastard!"

I slow down as the figure steps around the side of the building in front of me. They're silhouetted by the light coming from the van, but I can tell by their build and their looming presence that it's Maz. He must have double-backed on himself. Karen was just pretending to talk to him to throw me off. That bitch.

I stop and wait. He doesn't move. If he comes at me, I can maybe dummy around the side of him or slide through his legs. Or what if I jump in the water? Could I swim fast enough and get away? How cold would it be at this time of year?

I hunker down and ball up my fists. While I'm considering my options, I'm wasting time. I have to do something. Maz takes a step towards me and lets out a low rumbling laugh. My whole body is shaking, but I'm not done yet. He's not the only one who can play tricks. I make to run at him but as I put my foot forward, I push off against the ground and spin back around. And run straight into Karen coming the other way.

No!

I try to twist away from her, but she's too quick for me. She grabs a handful of my hair and pulls me back with such force I think for a second she's scalped me.

"You're a dickhead! Do you know that?" she hisses in my face.

I yell out as a burning pain spreads through my head. "Let me go!"

"Not a chance. You stupid bitch. Come on." She hustles me in front of her, still clutching my hair and shoves me forward. "Walk."

She marches me down the side of the building, yanking at

my hair every time I don't put one foot in front of the other quickly enough. I can feel the hard metal of her gun pressed into my spine. We get to the van and she pushes me against it. As I turn around it feels as if the world has closed in on me. She raises her gun and points it at my head.

"Now then," she snarls. "It's time we put an end to your meddling, Lauren Williams. Once and for all."

THIRTY-SEVEN

I hold my hands up in front of my face as Karen adjusts her grip on the gun handle. Even caught up in my heightened state of fear I can sense she has doubts. Maybe she hasn't killed anyone before. Maybe she's struggling with the task.

"Please, Karen. You don't have to do this."

"Shut up!" she snarls.

"Do it!" Maz calls out. "Or I will."

My eyes widen, heart pounding, as he pulls the gun from his jacket. This is it—the end. I'm about to die and there's no escape. Thoughts race through my mind, fighting for attention as time runs out. I think of Graham and my mother. I think again of Nana Mary and now of Peggy, too.

As my breath quickens, I close my eyes, seeking temporary solace from the nightmare. I raise my trembling arms in front of my chest, a pointless defence against the power of the gun, but it's all I've got. In the churning chaos of my thoughts, the instinct to survive wins out over the crushing weight of my fear.

A moment passes.

Then another.

Suddenly, to my left, the guttural roar of multiple car engines permeates the air, followed by the cacophony of screeching tires and protesting brakes.

"What the hell?" Karen's voice pierces the tension, her panic unmistakable. "Maz, what is it?"

I dare to open my eyes, catching sight of the burly man craning his neck to see over the van's roof. His already menacing scowl intensifies. "Police," he snarls, his voice dripping with contempt. "Fuck!"

What?

Did I just hear that correctly?

The police.

I lean forward as three cars pull up twenty yards away from us, bathing the area in bright halogen light. I screw up my eyes from the glare. I can hardly see what's going on. I hear doors opening and then shouting. Lots of shouting.

"Drop your weapons…!"

"Put down the guns…!"

Maz slams his body against the side of the van beside me. Then, before I know it, Karen is behind me with her arm around my throat.

"Get back," she yells, dragging me away from the van. "I'll kill her." To emphasise this point she jabs the end of her gun into the side of my head. It's cold and hard but I hardly notice it.

Maz steps out from behind the van and fires at the police. I scream and struggle against Karen's hold on me but she's too strong.

"Don't be stupid," she hisses in my ear. "I'll kill you right now."

Through the lights I can make out at least five or six figures, some are standing by their cars, others are crouched on the ground. They all look to be holding guns.

"Lay down your weapons and kneel with your arms in the air," someone shouts.

"Screw you," Maz shouts back. He looks over at Karen. "What do we do?"

I feel her shrug. "No idea. Can we get in the van? Get away?"

Maz sneers. "Nah. Screw it. I hate police."

"No!" Karen yells. She pulls me to one side so we both have a clear view of the big man as he steps away from the van and shoots at the rows of police cars. Almost instantly his huge frame is pummelled with return fire. I look down, watching through the corner of my eye as he dances and jerks on the spot for a few seconds before dropping to the floor.

"What the bloody hell are you doing!" Karen cries out. "You dickhead!"

"Let me go," I squeal. "You can still save yourself." I claw at her forearm, but she tightens her hold on me.

"Drop the gun!" a deep voice shouts.

Karen drags me backwards towards the warehouse, still with the gun at my head and positioning herself so I'm directly between her and the group of armed officers.

"Help me!" I cry out before Karen squeezes my neck so tight, I can't speak.

Everyone is shouting now but I can't tell what anyone is saying. Karen screams in my ear as she drags me away. She's panicked, I can tell. But why wouldn't she be? Her accomplice is dead, and she's got at least six trained firearm officers aiming guns at her. Or, rather, pointed at her via me. I have to change that. I have to do something.

"Get back," she yells at the police. "I will kill her. I mean it."

"Drop your weapon and release her."

"Piss off!"

She grinds the gun into my temple. She's frantic and desperate and people do silly things when they're frantic and desperate. All it takes is one squeeze of the trigger and I'm dead. I bite my lip, breathing heavily through my nostrils as I survey the scene. All my senses are on red alert. I can't breathe or construct any logical thoughts, but I know I have to do something. Do I trust myself? I have to. I will not die today. I sense the old Lauren rising inside of me. The part of me that was always wily and strong. The part of me that survived on instinct.

Karen is still moving away from the police, dragging me with her and yelling at them to back off. She moves the gun from my head and aims it at the police, swiping it across the line of cars before pointing it back at me. She does this once. Then she does it again a few seconds later. I straighten my legs and shift my weight forward, so she has to stop. She hisses something in my ear, but I can't tell what she says. I know she's spooked, unsure what to do. She slackens her hold on my neck and tries to adjust her grip, still screeching at the police that she's going to kill me. When they call back, she waves her gun at them in another desperate threat. And that's all I need. Grabbing my fist in my other hand I slam my elbow into her stomach. At the same time, I drop to my knees, becoming a dead weight and releasing myself from the headlock. I hit the ground and push off against her, falling backwards onto the concrete. The police yell. Karen screams. She points her gun at me and I close my eyes. Every muscle in my body is tight and ready. I hear gunshots. Many gunshots. I don't move. I can't. But I don't feel pain. I don't feel anything. Then, all at once, everything stops. I hear a dull thud a few feet away and open my eyes. It's Karen, lying on the ground in front of me. Her eyes and mouth are open but she's dead. The bullet hole in her forehead confirms this fact.

I hear someone cry out. It could be me. I don't know. I try to scramble away from Karen and Maz's fallen bodies. I want to get as far away from them as possible. Somehow, I get to my feet. People are shouting. I'm crying. I don't know what to do. I don't know where to go. I'm cold. I'm shaking.

What the hell is going on?

I can't hear…

I can't see…

My legs aren't working properly… I have an overriding impulse to run as fast as I can in any direction. But I'm certain if I try, I'm going to fall over…

As I stumble towards the light, I see people shouting and waving their arms at me.

"Get her away…"

"Someone grab her…"

A figure holds their arms out to me and as I reach the first police car a man rushes towards me and takes me by the hand.

"Lauren. You're in shock. But you're out of danger. Don't worry."

I shake my head as the man guides me away from the harsh lights towards the back of a parked police van. I'm out of danger. That's good to know. And this person. Do I know them? They sound familiar.

As my surroundings swim into focus, I'm able to think straighter. My heart is beating faster than I thought possible, and I'm soaked in a cold sweat, but I don't think I'm about to die any more. I gulp down a lungful of air and look up into Pete's smiling face.

"It's over, Lauren," he says. "You're safe."

THIRTY-EIGHT

Pete walks me over to an ambulance that has just pulled up and - while I'm examined by a friendly paramedic called Georgina – he explains what the hell has been going on for the past week. He tells me his real name is Mark Lamb and that he belongs to a special police unit who, for over a year, have been investigating the organised crime gang that Karen and Maz belonged to. It turns out the gang are into all sorts of nasty business: drugs, guns, human trafficking - and they use a lot of the houses in the area to run their operations. He confirms what Karen told me, that most of their properties are empty, but some have occupants, like the Cliftons, and that's when the cuckooing happens. So, I was right. They were taking advantage of Peggy and Ron. The bastards. Pete – or rather Mark – also explains that the gang rotate their stash houses and spare rooms and the properties that aren't being used are rented out via VayCay Rooms and similar sites. That way they cover their tracks, and no one gets wind of what they're up to. Or so they thought.

Georgina finishes shining a light in my eyes and gives my

shoulder a reassuring squeeze. I lean forward so I can see Mark properly as he stands in the doorway of the ambulance. "So, you've known something was wrong at Peggy's house for a while?" I ask him.

He gives a sheepish grin. "Yes. We've had eyes on some of the other gang members for months, but I only joined the task force recently. I was transferred here from another region and, as I wasn't known around the area, they put me straight on undercover surveillance. I was assigned Cranbourne Street where most of their stash houses are located. I've been watching number forty-seven specifically for the past three weeks."

"Right. I see." Georgina sits down next to me and rolls up my sleeve. My knuckles are grazed and weeping and there's a gash on my forearm which she dabs at with an iodine swab. It stings like hell, but I turn my attention back to Mark.

"When you arrived at the house and Peggy let you in, my unit went into overdrive," he says. "We were not expecting anyone like you to be involved. But we knew which websites the gang used to rent their properties and found your booking online. We had our best tech people find out who you were and what you were doing there. That's how I knew about your course. I'm sorry I couldn't say anything sooner. I wanted to. But it would have jeopardised the mission and we knew you were safe."

Georgina places a piece of gauze over the wound and starts wrapping a bandage around my arm.

"How did you know I was safe?" I ask.

Mark tilts his head and leans on the doorway. "Okay, we didn't know you were safe at *all* times. But we knew the old couple weren't a threat and if you moved – or if someone else moved you - we'd know." He nods his head back, gesturing behind him. "My colleague, Emily, over there was running surveillance today and saw you leave with Karen Andrews. She called for back-up straight away." I peer over to where he gestured but I can only see dark figures milling around. Emily must have been the person with the long hair I saw in the window.

"Was it not a bit risky?" I ask. "For me."

He grins, but it's a less sheepish grin than before. "We had it all under control. After Emily called it in, we employed the whole squad – including the armed response team. We followed you at a distance until we knew where you were heading."

"What if Karen had lost you."

"She wouldn't have done. I put a tracking app on your phone," he says. "It was when you went to the toilet in the pub the other night. I'm sorry to be all cloak and dagger about it. Like I say, I wanted to tell you. But you've already provided us with useful information that will hopefully lead to some arrests. Are you willing to make a statement about what happened tonight? With that and other intel we've gained recently, we think we can nail the big boss. A man called Shane Daglish. He's a nasty bastard. He runs county lines gangs across most of the north."

I nod. A part of me wants to make him work for it a bit more, but I already know I'll cooperate. "Fine," I say. "I'll do whatever I have to if it means those bastards don't prey on any more vulnerable people like Peggy and Ron. By the way, they aren't in trouble, are they?"

He shakes his head, and a heavy silence descends over the scene. Georgina finishes dressing my wounds and stands up to flick through a clipboard of papers. I watch her for a moment then turn back to Mark.

"Was it all bullshit?" I ask him. "Everything you told me?"

His brow crumples. "What do you mean? I'm not called Pete…"

"About your past. About having gone through a bad break-up. Did you say that just because you knew about me and wanted to *connect*?"

"No. It wasn't bullshit." He glances at Georgina. She's got her back to him but is probably listening to our conversation. She is only human, after all. I look at Mark, nodding for him to go on. He smiles. "I have recently broken up with someone and I honestly didn't know you had until we started talking. That was all just a coincidence. And it was all true. I moved up here to get away from my old life down in Sussex. I enjoyed talking to you that night in the pub. It was nice."

He looks down and I see something in his face that tells me he's still the man I thought – or rather, hoped - he was. I can't believe I thought he could be involved. He's a good person. He was always a good person. And I need to start listening to my gut again. Because I'm a good person too.

Mark raises his head and smiles. I smile back. It's sort of awkward but sort of nice. Behind me, I sense Georgina is also smiling to herself.

"I'll let you finish off here and then I'll give you a lift down to the station. It's best if we get a statement from you tonight. Is that okay?"

"No problem," I say as he goes to walk off, but then something comes to me. "Oh, by the way. Pe—Mark!"

He stops. "Yeah?"

"My suitcase. It's in the boot of the Ford Fiesta. And Karen took my phone. Can you…?"

He winks at me. "I'll recover them. Don't worry."

———

It's a few minutes after ten when I finish at the police station. I've made a lengthy statement and have told the interviewing officers everything I saw and experienced over the last week. They seem pleased with what I've told them and take down my details in case I'm needed at the trial. Their hope is they'll have enough evidence on the gang it won't come to that but, regardless I'm prepared. It will be scary as hell to have to stand in the dock and say these things in front of dangerous people, but I can handle it. I'm Lauren Williams. I can handle anything.

Once I'm signed out at the front desk, I wander through the double doors and out into the car park. The night is still and the air is cool, but it perks me up. I feel alive. I feel good. I was planning on getting a taxi to The Gilded Griffin, but Mark stopped me in the corridor after I'd finished my interview and insisted that he would give me a lift. He said it's the least he could do, after everything I've been through, and I suppose that's fair enough.

I asked him if I'd be able to see Peggy and Ron before I go back to Manchester, but he said it was probably a bad idea. Maybe I'll come back to visit them once the local gang members are locked up and out of the picture. I doubt Ron would remember me, but Peggy might. I'd like to say goodbye to her properly and tell her I'm sorry. Not that any of this was my fault but I am sorry she's had to endure what she has done. Losing a child has to be the worst thing that can ever happen to a parent, but then to have these awful people invade her home. She's a nice person and she doesn't deserve any of the crap life has thrown at her.

"There you are, I was beginning to think you'd run off."

I turn around to see Mark standing behind me. I must have jumped because he raises his hands. "Sorry, I didn't mean to scare you."

I smile. "One of those nights." He has my suitcase with him and my phone in his other hand.

"Here. I found it." He hands it to me. It's still switched on but as I swipe at the screen, I see the battery is low. That's fine. I've got a charger in my suitcase and there's enough battery life for what I need to do. I open up my contacts list and find Graham's name. This time I don't hesitate and hit the delete button before confirming my request. That's it. He's gone. The bastard is out of my life. And it feels good. It feels even better when I delete our message thread on WhatsApp. I'll delete him from social media later when I've more time.

"I'm parked just over there," Mark says, pointing across the car park. It's the same car in which he gave me a life to Samstone Manor.

"Are you sure you don't mind driving me?" I ask as we walk over.

"I offered, didn't I? My guv just told me to get off home, so I'm free for the rest of the night. It's no problem."

He unlocks the car with his key fob before we reach it, but still hurries ahead and opens the passenger door for me.

"Why, thank you," I say. "What a gentleman."

He shrugs in a show of mock humility. "I do my best."

I chuckle to myself as I climb into the car, and he closes the door after me. As he puts my case in the boot, I get comfortable and pull the seat belt across me before letting out a long sigh. It feels as if all the tension I've been carrying with me this last week leaves in one go.

What a crazy week.

I still don't know how I feel about everything that's

happened but for now, I'm staying focused on the present. I expect there'll be a point in a few days when the extent of how much danger I was in hits me, but I'll deal with that when it happens. It'll take more than those pricks - and Graham - to get me down.

I had wondered about calling in sick tomorrow and not attending the last day of my course – I don't think anyone would blame me if I did - but I've decided I want to see it through. This is why I'm here, after all. This is the start of my new life.

How's about that for resilience, ability to adapt and team spirit, Rochelle?

What I do plan on doing, however, is booking an extra night at The Gilded Griffin and taking the next day off work as a personal day. I don't imagine Rochelle will mind granting me one more days leave when she finds out what happened here. I plan on sleeping late, having a decent breakfast, and then maybe going for a walk in the countryside near the hotel. There's a lot of beautiful scenery around here - if you look in the right direction. And maybe that's true of life as well.

Mark climbs into the driver's seat alongside me and starts the engine. "Right then, Miss Williams let's get you to your hotel. The Gilded Griffin, yes?"

I lean back against the headrest and look at him. "That's the one. Unless…?"

He frowns. "Unless what?"

"You said you've just got off the night," I say, glancing at the clock on the dashboard. "I don't suppose you want to get a last drink?"

He arches one eyebrow. "Are you sure? After tonight, I can understand a stiff drink might be helpful, but shouldn't you rest? You've been through a lot."

I shrug. "Mark, my life has always been chaotic. It'll take more than Karen and her mate to stop me."

He grins. "If you're sure."

"I'm sure," I tell him. "But this time, let's go somewhere decent, okay? Not like that dive you took me to last time."

"Fair enough."

He laughs and so do I. And it's a real laugh, from deep inside of me. The sort of laugh that fills you with energy and makes you believe that life could be okay after all. It feels good. It's freeing.

It's been a long time.

THE END

———

Want more? Get your free novel:

THE EX

What if you found out your ex-boyfriend's former lovers were all dying in mysterious circumstances, and you were next on the list?

Get your FREE copy by clicking here

———

Enjoy psychological & domestic thrillers?
You'll love…

THE PACT

"We had a pact and I broke it. That's why she hates me. That's why she's tracked me down. That's why she wants to make me pay…"

<u>Get your copy by clicking here</u>

CAN YOU HELP?

Enjoyed this book? You can make a big difference

Honest reviews of my books help bring them to the attention of other readers. If you've enjoyed this book I would be so grateful if you could spend just five minutes leaving a comment (it can be as short as you like) on the book's Amazon page.

ALSO BY M. I. HATTERSLEY

THE DEMAND

Your phone rings. A distorted voice tells you they've taken your daughter. They will kill her unless you carry out their demand. You have two days...

CLICK HERE TO GET YOUR COPY

———

ABOUT THE AUTHOR

M I Hattersley is a bestselling author of psychological & domestic thrillers and crime fiction.

He lives with his wife and young daughter in Derbyshire, UK

Printed in Great Britain
by Amazon